Dear Anthony,

We hope you enjoy this book. It is a reprint of one printed probably in the early 1930's — written in the style of books for boys in those years.

Love,
Geo and Dona

Dave Darrin's Second Year at Annapolis

H. Irving Hancock

Table of Contents

Dave Darrin's Second Year at Annapolis

H. Irving Hancock

Kessinger Publishing reprints thousands of hard–to–find books!

```
Dave Darrin's Second Year at Annapolis
        Or, Two Midshipmen as Naval Academy "Youngsters"
```

[Illustration: Darrin's Blow Knocked the Midshipman Down]

DAVE DARRIN'S SECOND YEAR AT ANNAPOLIS

or

Two Midshipmen as Naval Academy "Youngsters"

By

H. IRVING HANCOCK Illustrated

MCMXI

CHAPTER I. A QUESTION OF MIDSHIPMAN HONOR

"How can a midshipman and gentleman act in that way?"

The voice of Midshipman David Darrin, United States Navy, vibrated uneasily as he turned to his comrades.

"It's a shame—that's what it is," quivered Mr. Farley, also of the third class at the United States Naval Academy.

"But the question is," propounded Midshipman Dan Dalzell, "what are we going to do about it?"

"Is it any part of our business to bother with the fellow?" demanded Farley half savagely.

Now Farley was rather hot—tempered, though he was "all there" in points that involved the honor of the brigade of midshipmen.

Five midshipmen stood in the squalid, ill—odored back room of a Chinese laundry in the town of Annapolis.

Dave Darrin's Second Year at Annapolis

There was a sixth midshipman present in the handsome blue uniform of the brigade; and it was upon this sixth one that the anger and disgust of the other five had centered.

He lay in a sleep too deep for stirring. On the still, foul air floated fumes that were new to those of his comrades who now gazed down on him.

"To think that one of our class could make such a beast of himself!" sighed Dave Darrin.

"And on the morning of the very day we're to ship for the summer cruise," uttered Farley angrily.

"Oh, well" growled Hallam, "why not let this animal of lower grade sleep just where he is? Let him take what he has fairly brought upon himself!"

"That's the very question that is agitating me," declared Dave Darrin, to whom these other members of the third class looked as a leader when there was a point involving class honor.

Dave had became a leader through suffering.

Readers of the preceding volume in this series, "DAVE DARRIN'S FIRST YEAR AT ANNAPOLIS," will need no introduction to this fine specimen of spirited and honorable young American.

Readers of that preceding volume will recall how Dave Darrin and Dan Dalzell entered the United States Naval Academy, one appointed by a Congressman and the other by a United States Senator. Such readers will remember the difficult time that Dave and Dan had in getting through the work of the first hard, grinding year. They will also recall how Dave Darrin, when accused of treachery to his classmates, patiently bided his time until he, with the aid of some close friends, was able to demonstrate his innocence. Our readers will also remember how two evil—minded members of the then fourth class plotted to increase Damn's disgrace and to drive him out of the brigade; also how these two plotters, Midshipmen Henkel and Brimmer, were caught in their plotting and were themselves forced out of the brigade. Our readers know that before the end of the first year at the Naval Academy, Dave had fully reinstated himself in the esteem of his manly classmates, and how he quickly became the most popular and respected member of his class.

Dave Darrin's Second Year at Annapolis

It was now only the day after the events whose narration closed the preceding volume.

Dave Darrin and Dalzell were first of all brought to notice in "THE HIGH SCHOOL BOYS' SERIES." In their High School days, back in Gridley, these two had been famous members of Dick &Co., a sextette of youngsters who had made a name for themselves in school athletics.

Dick Prescott and Greg Holmes, two other members of the sextette, had been appointed to the United States Military Academy at West Point, where they were serving in the corps of cadets and learning how to become Army officers in the not far distant future. All of the adventures of Dick and Greg are set forth in "THE WEST POINT SERIES."

The two remaining members of famous old Dick &Co., Tom Reade and Harry Hazelton, became civil engineers, and went West for their first taste of engineering work. Tom and Harry had some wonderful and startling adventures, as fully set forth in "THE YOUNG ENGINEERS' SERIES."

On this early June day when we again encounter Dave Darrin and Dan Dalzell in their handsome Naval uniforms, all members of the first, second and third classes were due to be aboard one of the three great battleships that lay off the Yard at Annapolis at four p.m.

These three great battleships were the "Massachusetts," the "Iowa" and the "Indiana." These three huge, turreted fighting craft had their full crews aboard. Not one of the battleship commanders would allow a "jackie" ashore, except on business, through fear that many of the "wilder" ones might find the attractions on shore too alluring, and fail to return in time.

With the young midshipmen it was different. These young men were officially and actually gentlemen, and could be trusted.

Yet here, in the back room of this laundry, was one who was apparently not dependable.

This young midshipman's name was Pennington, and the fact was that he lay in deep stupor from the effects of smoking opium!

4

It had been a storekeeper, with a shop across the street, who had called the attention of Dave and his four comrades to the probable fate of another of their class.

"Chow Hop runs a laundry, but I have heard evil stories about a lot of young fools who flock to his back room and get a chance to 'hit' the opium pipe," the storekeeper had stated to Dave. "One of your men, or at least, one in a midshipman's uniform, went in there at eleven o'clock this forenoon, and he hasn't been out since. It is now nearly two o'clock and, I've been looking for some midshipmen to inform."

Such had been the storekeeper's careful statement. The merchants of Annapolis always have a kindly feeling toward these fine young midshipmen. The storekeeper's purpose was to enable them to help their comrade out.

So the five had entered the laundry. The proprietor, Chow Hop, had attempted to bar their way to the rear room.

But Dave had seized the yellow man and had flung him aside.

The reader already knows what they discovered, and how it affected these young men.

"Bring that copper—colored chink in here, if you'll be so good," directed Dave.

Dan and Hallam departed on the quest.

"You're wanted in there," proclaimed Dalzell, jerking a thumb over his shoulder.

"Me no sabby," replied Chow Hop, looking up briefly from his ironing board.

"Get in there—do you hear?" commanded Hallam, gripping the other's arm with all his force.

"You lemme go chop—chop (quickly), or you get alle samee hurt—you sabby?" scowled Chow Hop, using his free hand to raise a heavy flat—iron menacingly.

But Dan Dalzell jumped in, giving the Chinaman's wrist a wrench that caused him to drop the iron.

Then, without a bit of ceremony, Dan grasped the Oriental by the shoulders, wheeled him about, while he protested in guttural tones, and bluntly kicked the yellow–faced one through the door into the inner room.

At this summary proceeding both the Chinese helpers gripped their flat–irons firmly; and leaped forward to fight.

In an ugly temper the Chinaman is a bad man to oppose. But now this pair were faced by a pair of quietly smiling midshipmen who were also dangerous when angry.

"You two, get back," ordered Dalzell, advancing fearlessly upon the pair. "If you don't, we'll drag you out into the street and turn you over to the policemen. You 'sabby' that? You heathen are pretty likely to get into prison for this day's work!"

Scowling for a moment, then muttering savagely, the two helpers slunk back to their ironing boards.

Yet, while Dan turned to go into the rear room, Hallam stood just where he was, to keep an eye on two possible sources of swift trouble.

"Chow Hop," began Dave Damn sternly, as the proprietor made his flying appearance, "You've done a pretty mean piece of work here"—pointing to the unconscious midshipman in the berth. "Do you understand that you're pretty likely to go to prison for this?"

"Oh, that no maller," replied Chow, with a sullen grin. "Him plenty 'shipmen come here and smoke."

"You lie!" hissed Dave, grasping the heathen by the collar and shaking him until the latter's teeth rattled.

Then Dave gave him a brief rest, though he still retained his hold on the Chinaman's collar. But the yellow man began struggling again, and Dave repeated the shaking.

Chow Hop had kept his hands up inside his wide sleeves. Now Farley leaped forward as he shouted:

"Look out, Darry! He has a knife!"

Farley attempted to seize the Chinaman's wrist, for the purpose of disarming the yellow man, but Dave swiftly threw the Chinaman around out of Farley's reach. Then, with a lightning-like move, Dave knocked the knife from Chow Hop's hand.

"Pick that up and keep it for a curio, Farley," directed Dave coolly.

In another twinkling Darrin had run the Chinaman up against the wall.

Smack! biff! thump!

With increasing force Dave's hard fist struck the heathen in the face.

"Now stand there and behave yourself," admonished Midshipman Dave, dropping his hold on the yellow man's collar, "or we'll stop playing with you and hurt you some."

The scowl on Chow Hop's face was ominous, but he stood still, glaring at Dave.

"Chow, what can we do to bring this man out of his sleep!" asked Dave coolly, and almost in a friendly tone.

"Me no sabby," sulked the Chinaman.

"Yes, you do," retorted Dave warningly. "Now, what can we do to get our friend out of this!"

"You allee same cally (carry) him out," retorted Chow, with a suspicion of a sulky grin.

"None of that, now, you yellow-face!" glared Dave. "How shall we get our comrade out of this opium sleep!"

"Me no sabby no way," insisted Chow.

"Oh, yes, you do!" snapped Dave. "But you won't tell. All right; we'll find the way, and we'll punish you into the bargain. Dan, get a piece of paper from the other room."

7

Dalzell was quickly back with the desired item. On the paper Dave wrote a name and a telephone number.

"It's near the end of the doctor's office hours," murmured Dave. "Go to a telephone and ask the doctor to meet you at the corner above. Tell him it's vastly important, and ask him to meet you on the jump."

"Shall I tell him what's up!" asked Dan cautiously.

"Yes; you'd better. Then he'll be sure to bring the necessary remedies with him."

Dan Dalzell was off like a shot.

Chow tried to edge around toward the door.

"Here, you get back there," cried Dave, seizing the Chinaman and slamming him back against the wall. "Don't you move again, until we tell you that you may—or it will be the worse for you."

Ten minutes passed ere Dan returned with Dr. Lawrence.

"You see the job that's cut out for you," said Darrin, pointing to the unconscious figure in the bunk. "Can you do it, Doctor?"

The medical man made a hasty examination of the unconscious midshipman before he answered briefly:

"Yes."

"Will it be a long job, Doctor?"

"Fifteen minutes, probably."

"Oh, good, if you can do it in that time!"

"Me go now?" asked Chow, with sullen curiosity, as the medical man opened his medicine-case.

"Yes; if you don't try to leave the joint," agreed Dave. "And I'm going outside with you."

Chow looked very much as though he did not care for company, but Midshipman Darrin kept at his side.

"Now, see here, Chow," warned Dave, "this is the last day you sell opium for white men to smoke!"

"You heap too flesh (fresh)" growled the Chinaman.

"It's the last day you'll sell opium to white men," insisted Dave, "for, as soon as I'm through here I'm going to the police station to inform against you. They'll go through here like a twelve-inch shot."

"You alle same tell cop?" grinned Chow, green hatred showing through his skin. "Then I tell evelybody about you fliend in there."

"Do just as you please about that," retorted Dave with pretended carelessness. "For one thing, you don't know his name."

"Oh, yes, I do," swaggered Chow impudently. "Know heap 'bout him. His name alle same Pen'ton."

Seizing a marking brush and a piece of paper, Chow Hop quickly wrote out Pennington's name, correctly spelled. His ability to write English with a good hand was one of Chow's great vanities, anyway.

"You go back to your ironing board, yellow-face," warned Darrin, and something in the young third classman's face showed Chow that it would be wise to obey.

Then Hallam drew Darrin to one side, to whisper earnestly in his ear:

"Look out, old man, or you will get Pen into an awful scrape!"

"I shan't do it," maintained Darrin. "If it happens it will have been Pen's own work."

"You'd better let the chink go, just to save one of our class."

"Is a fellow who has turned opium fiend worth saving to the class!" demanded Dave, looking straight into Hallam's eyes.

"Well, er—er—" stammered the other man.

"You see," smiled Dave, "the doubt hits you just as hard as it does me!"

"Oh, of course, a fellow who has turned opium fiend is no fellow ever to be allowed to reach the bridge and the quarter—deck," admitted Hallam. "But see here, are you going to report this affair to the commandant of midshipmen, or to anyone else in authority?"

"I've no occasion to report," replied Dave dryly. "I am not in any way in command over Pennington. But I mean to persuade him to report himself for what he has done!"

"But that would ruin him!" protested Hallam, aghast. "He wouldn't even be allowed to start on the cruise. He'd be railroaded home without loss of a moment."

"Yet you've just said that an opium—user isn't fit to go on in the brigade," retorted Darrin.

"Hang it, it's hard to know what to do," rejoined Hallam, wrinkling his forehead. "Of course we want to be just to Pen."

"It doesn't strike me as being just exactly a question of justice to Pennington," Darrin went on earnestly. "If this is anything it's a question of midshipman honor. We fellows are bound to see that all the unworthy ones are dropped from the service. Now, a fellow who has fastened the opium habit on himself isn't fit to go on, is he?"

"Oh, say, but this is a hard one to settle!" groaned Hallam.

"Then I'll take all the responsibility upon myself," said Dave promptly. "I don't want to make any mistake, and I don't believe I'm going to. Wait just a moment."

Going to the rear room, Dave faced his three comrades there with the question:

"You three are enough to take care of everything here for a few minutes, aren't you?"

"Yes," nodded Dan. "What's up?"

"Hallam and I are going for a brief walk."

Then, stepping back into the front room, Darrin nodded to his classmate, who followed him outside.

"Just come along, and say nothing about the matter on the street," requested Dave. "It might be overheard."

"Where are you going?" questioned Hallam wonderingly.

"Wait and see, please."

From Chow Hop's wretched establishment it was not far to the other building that Dave had in mind as a destination.

But when they arrived, and stood at the foot of the steps, Hallam clutched Darrin's arm, holding him back.

"Why, see here, this is the police station!"

"I know it," Dave replied calmly.

"But see here, you're not—"

"I'm not going to drag you into anything that you'd object to," Darrin continued. "Come along; all I want you for is as a witness to what I am going to say."

"Don't do it, old fel—"

"I've thought that over, and I feel that I must," replied Dave firmly. "Come along. Don't attract attention by standing here arguing."

In another instant the two midshipmen were going swiftly up the steps.

The chief of police received his two callers courteously. Dave told the official how their attention had been called to the fact that one of their number was in an opium joint. Dave named the place, but requested the chief to wait a full hour before taking any action.

"That will give us a chance to get out a comrade who may have committed only his first offense," Dave continued.

"If there's any opium being smoked in that place I'll surely close the joint out!" replied the chief, bringing his fist down upon his desk. "But I understand your reasons, Mr.—"

"Darrin is my name, sir," replied Dave quietly.

"So, Mr. Darrin, I give you my word that I won't even start my investigations before this evening. And I'll keep all quiet about the midshipman end of it."

"Thank you very much, sir," said Dave gratefully.

As the two midshipmen strolled slowly back in the direction of Chow Hop's, Dave murmured:

"Now, you see why I took this step?"

"I'm afraid not very clearly," replied Midshipman Hallam.

"That scoundrelly Chow made his boast that other midshipmen patronized his place. I don't believe it. Such a vice wouldn't appeal to you, and it doesn't to me. But there are more than two hundred new plebes coming in just now, and many of these boys have never been away from home before. Some of them might foolishly seek the lure of a new vice, and might find the habit fastened on them before they were aware of it. Chow's vile den might spoil some good material for the quarter–deck, and, as a matter of midshipman honor, we're bound to see that the place is cleaned out right away."

12

"I guess, Darry, you come pretty near being right," assented Hallam, after thinking for a few moments.

By the time they reached Chow Hop's again they found that Dr. Lawrence had brought the unfortunate Pennington to. And a very scared and humiliated midshipman it was who now stood up, a bit unsteadily, and tried to smooth down his uniform.

"How do you feel now?" asked Dave.

"Awful!" shuddered Pennington. "And now see here, what are you fellows going to do? Blab, and see me driven out of the Navy?"

"Don't do any talking in here," advised Dave, with a meaning look over his shoulder at the yellow men in the outer room. "Doctor, is our friend in shape to walk along with us now?"

"He will be, in two or three minutes, after he drinks something I'm going to give him," replied the medical man, shaking a few drops from each of three vials into a glass of water. "Here, young man, drink this slowly."

Three minutes later the midshipmen left the place, Dave walking beside Pennington and holding his arm lightly for the purpose of steadying him.

"How did this happen, Pen?" queried Dave, when the six men of the third class at last found themselves walking down Maryland Avenue. "How long have you been at this 'hop' trick?"

"Never before to–day," replied Midshipman Pennington quickly.

"Pen, will you tell me that on your honor?" asked Dave gravely.

The other midshipman flared up.

"Why must I give you my word of honor?" he demanded defiantly. "Isn't my plain word good enough?"

"Your word of honor that you had never smoked opium before to-day would help to ease my mind a whole lot," replied Darrin. "Come, unburden yourself, won't you, Pen?"

"I'll tell you, Darry, just how it happened. To-day *was* the first time, on my word of honor, I came out into Annapolis with a raging toothache. Now, you know how a fellow gets to hate to go before the medical officers of the Academy with a tale about his teeth."

"Yes, I do," nodded Darrin. "If a fellow is too much on the medical report for trouble with his teeth, then it makes the surgeons look his mouth over with all the more caution, and in the end a fellow may get dropped from the brigade just because he has invited over zeal from the dentist. But what has all this to do with opium smoking?"

"Just this," replied Pennington, hanging his head. "I went into a drug store and asked a clerk that I know what was the best thing for toothache. He told me the best he knew was to smoke a pipe of opium, and told me where to find Chow Hop, and what to say to the chink. And it's all a lie about opium helping a sore tooth," cried the wretched midshipman, clapping a hand to his jaw, "for there goes that fiendish tooth again! But say! You fellows are not going to leak about my little mishap?"

"No," replied Darrin with great promptness. "You're going to do that yourself."

"What?" gasped Midshipman Pennington in intense astonishment. "What are you talking about?"

"You'll be wise to turn in a report, on what happened," pursued Dave, "for it's likely to reach official ears, anyway, and you'll be better off if you make the first report on the subject."

"Why is it likely to reach official ears, if you fellows keep your mouths shut?"

"You see," Darrin went on very quietly, "I reported the joint at the police station, and Chow Hop threatened that, if I did, he'd tell all he knew about everybody. So you'd better be first——"

"You broke the game out to the police!" gasped Pennington, staring dumfoundedly at his comrade. "What on earth——"

"I did it because I had more than one satisfactory reason for considering it my duty," interposed Dave, speaking quietly though firmly.

"You—you—bag of wind!" exploded Midshipman Pennington.

"I'll accept your apology when you've had time to think it all over," replied Dave, with a smile, though there was a brief flash in his eyes.

"I'll make no apology to you—at any time, you—you—greaser!"

Marks for efficiency or good conduct, which increase a midshipman's standing, are called "grease–marks" or "grease" in midshipman slang. Hence a midshipman who is accused of currying favor with his officers in order to win "grease" is contemptuously termed a "greaser."

"I don't want to talk with you any more, Mr. Darrin," Pennington went on bitterly, "or walk with you, either. When I get over this toothache I'll call you out—you greaser!"

Burning with indignation, Midshipman Pennington fell back to walk with Hallam.

CHAPTER II. DAVE'S PAP–SHEET ADVICE

When our party reached the landing a lively scene lay before them.

Fully a hundred midshipmen, belonging to the first, second and third classes, were waiting to be transported out to one or another of the great, gray battleships.

Several launches were darting back and forth over the water. The baggage of the midshipmen had already been taken aboard the battleships. Only the young men themselves were now awaited.

Near–by stood a lieutenant of the Navy, who was directing the embarkation of the midshipmen of the different classes.

Five minutes after our party arrived a launch from the "Massachusetts" lay in alongside the landing.

"Third classmen, this way!" shouted the lieutenant. "How many of you?"

Turning his eyes over the squad that had moved forward, the officer continued:

"Twenty–two. You can all crowd into this launch. Move quickly, young gentlemen!"

In another couple of minutes the puffing launch was steaming away to the massive battleship that lay out in the stream.

Dave stood well up in the bow. Once he barely overheard Pennington mutter to a comrade:

"The rascally greaser!"

"That means me," Dave muttered under his breath. "I won't take it up now, or in any hurry. I'll wait until Pen has had time to see things straight."

As soon as the launch lay alongside, the young midshipmen clambered nimbly up the side gangway, each raising his cap to the flag at the stern as he passed through the opening in the rail.

Here stood an officer with an open book in his hand. To him each midshipman reported, saluting, stated his name, and received his berthing.

"Hurry away to find your berthings, and get acquainted with the location," ordered this officer. "Every midshipman will report on the quarter–deck promptly at five p.m. In the meantime, after locating your berthings, you are at liberty to range over the ship, avoiding the ward room and the staterooms of officers."

The latest arrivals saluted. Then, under the guidance of messengers chosen from among the apprentice members of the crew, the young men located their berthings.

"I'm going to get mine changed, if I can," growled Pennington, wheeling upon Dave Darrin. "I'm much too close to a greaser. I'm afraid I may get my uniforms spotted, as well as my character."

"Stop that, Pen!" warned Dave, stationing himself squarely before the angry Pennington. "I don't know just how far you're responsible for what you're saying now. To—morrow, if you make any such remarks to me, you'll have to pay a mighty big penalty for them."

"You'll make me pay by going to the commandant and telling him all you know, I suppose?" sneered Pennington.

"You know better, Pen! Now, begin to practise keeping a civil tongue behind your teeth!"

With that, Darrin turned on his heel, seeking the deck.

This left "Pen" to conjecture as to whether he should report his misadventure, and, if so, how best to go about it.

"See here, Hallam," began the worried midshipman, "I begin to feel that it will be safer to turn in some kind of report on myself."

"Much safer," agreed Hallam. "It will show good faith on your part if you report yourself."

"And get me broken from the service, too, I suppose," growled the unhappy one.

"I hardly think it will, if you report yourself first," urged Hallam. "But you'll be about certain to get your walking papers if you wait for the first information to come from other sources."

"Hang it," groaned Pennington, "I wish I could think, but my head aches as though it would split and my tooth is putting up more trouble than I ever knew there was in the world. And, in this racked condition, I'm to go and put myself on the pap—sheet. In what way shall I do it, Hallam? Can't you suggest something?"

"Yes," retorted Hallam with great energy. "Go to the medical officer and tell him how your tooth troubles you. Tell him what you tried on shore. I'll go with you, if you want."

"Will you, old man? I'll be a thousand times obliged!"

So the pair went off in search of the sick—bay, as the hospital part of a battleship is called. The surgeon was not in his office adjoining, but the hospital steward called him over one of the ship telephones, informing him that a midshipman was suffering with an ulcerated tooth.

Dr. Mackenzie came at once, turned on a reflector light, and gazed into Midshipman Pennington's mouth.

"Have you tried to treat this tooth yourself, in any way?" queried the ship's surgeon.

"Yes, sir; I was so crazy with the pain, while in Annapolis, that I am afraid I did something that will get me into trouble," replied Pennington, with a quiver in his voice.

"What was that?" asked Dr. Mackenzie, glancing at him sharply. "Did you try the aid of liquor?"

"Worse, I'm afraid, sir."

"Worse?"

Pennington told of his experience with the opium pipe.

"That's no good whatever for a toothache, sir," growled Dr. Mackenzie. "Besides, it's a serious breach of discipline. I shall have to report you, Mr. Pennington."

"I expected it, sir," replied Pennington meekly.

"However, the report won't cure your toothache," continued Dr. Mackenzie in a milder tone. "We'll attend to that first."

The surgeon busied himself with dissolving a drug in a small quantity of water. This he took up in a hypodermic needle and injected into the lower jaw.

"The ache ought to stop in ten minutes, sir," continued the surgeon, turning to enter some memoranda in his record book.

After that the surgeon called up the ship's commander over the 'phone, and made known Pennington's report.

"Mr. Pennington, Captain Scott directs that you report at his office immediately," said the surgeon, as he turned away from the telephone.

"Very good, sir. Thank you, sir."

Both midshipmen saluted, then left the sick–bay.

"This is where you have to go up alone, I guess," hinted Midshipman Hallam.

"I'm afraid so," sighed Pennington.

"However, I'll be on the quarter–deck, and, if I'm wanted, you can send there for me."

"Thank you, old man. You're worth a brigade of Darrins—confound the greasing meddler!"

"Darrin acted according to his best lights on the subject of duty," remonstrated Mr. Hallam mildly.

"His best lights—bah!" snarled Pennington. "I'll take this all out of him before I'm through with him!"

Pennington reported to the battleship's commander. After some ten minutes a marine orderly found Hallam and directed him to go to Captain Scott's office. Here Hallam repeated as much as was asked of him concerning the doings of the afternoon. Incidentally, the fact of Midshipman Darrin's report to the police was brought out.

"Mr. Pennington, I shall send you at once, in a launch, over to the commandant of cadets to report this matter in person to him," said Captain Scott gravely. "Mr. Hallam, you will go with Mr. Pennington."

Then, after the two had departed, an apprentice messenger went through the ship calling Dave's name. That young man was summoned to Captain Scott's office.

"I am in possession of all the facts relating to the unfortunate affair of Midshipman Pennington, Mr. Darrin," began Captain Scott, after the interchange of salutes. "Will you tell me why you reported the affair to the police?"

"I went to the police, sir," Dave replied, "because I was aware that many members of the new fourth class are away from home for the first time in their lives. I was afraid, sir, that possibly some of the new midshipmen might, during one of their town-leaves, be tempted to try for a new experience."

"A very excellent reason, Mr. Darrin, and I commend you heartily for it. I shall also report your exemplary conduct to the commandant of midshipmen. You have, in my opinion, Mr. Darrin, displayed very good judgment, and you acted upon that judgment with promptness and decision. But I am afraid," continued the Navy captain dryly, "that you have done something that will make you highly unpopular, for a while, with some of the members of your class."

"I hope not, sir," replied Dave.

"So do I," smiled Captain Scott "I am willing to find myself a poor prophet. That is all, Mr. Darrin."

Once more saluting, Dave left the commanding officer's presence. Almost the first classmate into whom he stumbled was Dan Dalzell.

"Well, from what quarter does the wind blow!" murmured Dan.

Darrin repeated the interview that he had just had.

"I'm afraid, Dave, little giant, that you've planted something of a mine under yourself," murmured Dalzell.

"I feel as much convinced as ever, Danny boy, that I did just what I should have done," replied Darrin seriously.

"And so does Captain Scott, and so will the commandant," replied Dan. "But winning the commendation of your superior officers doesn't always imply that you'll get much praise from your classmates."

"Unfortunately, you are quite right," smiled Dave. "Still, I'd do the same thing over again."

"Oh, of course you would," assented Dan. "That's because you're Dave Darrin."

Here a voice like a bass horn was heard.

"All third classmen report to the quarter–deck immediately!"

This order was repeated in other parts of the ship. Midshipmen gathered with a rush, Pennington and Hallam being the only members absent. As soon as the third classmen, or "youngsters," as they are called in midshipman parlance, had formed, the orders were read off dividing them into sections for practical instruction aboard ship during the cruise.

Dave's name was one of the first read off. He was assigned to duty as section leader for the first section in electrical instruction. Dalzell, Farley, Hallam, Pennington and others were detailed as members of that section.

The same section was also designated for steam instruction, Dalzell being made leader of the section in this branch.

The class was then dismissed. Somewhat later Pennington and Hallam returned from their interview with the commandant.

Hallam at once sought out Dave.

"Darry, old man," murmured Hallam, "Pen is as crazy as a hornet against you. As he had taken the first step by sticking himself on the pap–sheet (placing himself on report), the commandant said he would make the punishment a lighter one."

"What did Pen get?" queried Dave.

"Fifty demerits, with all the loss of privileges that fifty carry."

"He's lucky," declared Dave promptly. "Had the report come from other sources, he would have been dismissed from the service."

"If Pen's lucky," rejoined Hallam, "he doesn't seem to realize the fact. He's calling you about everything."

"He can keep that up," flashed Dave, "until his toothache leaves him. Then, if he tries to carry it any further, Pen will collide with one of my fists!"

Not much later a call sounded summoning the youngsters to the midshipmen's mess. Dave was glad to note that Pennington sat at some distance from him at table.

While the meal was in progress the "Massachusetts" and the other battleships got under way. The midshipmen were on deck, an hour later, when the fleet came to anchor for the night, some miles down Chesapeake Bay.

Before the youngsters were ordered to their berths that night Third Classman Pennington had found opportunity to do a good deal of talking to a few comrades who would listen to him.

Pennington was determined to stir up a hornet's nest for Dave Darrin.

CHAPTER III. MIDSHIPMAN PENNINGTON GOES TOO FAR

At eight o'clock the following morning the various sections were formed and marched to the deck.

Dave reported:

"All present, sir."

The chief electrician was now summoned, and to him the section was turned over. This young man, Whittam, by name, was an enlisted man, but a bright young sample of what the Navy can do for the boy who enlists as an apprentice.

"You will take your orders from Mr. Whittam as though he were an officer," directed the officer, his words intended for all members of the section, though he looked only at Darrin.

Dave saluted, then, as Chief Electrician Whittam turned to lead the way, Dave called quietly:

"Section, left wheel—march!"

They followed Whittam down into the dynamo room, an interesting spot for a machinist.

"It's fine," muttered Dan, as he stared about him at the bright metal work, the switch–board and the revolving machines. "But I'm afraid I couldn't learn the use and sense of all this in five years."

"Silence in the section," commanded Dave, turning around upon his chum.

Whittam now began a short, preliminary talk upon the subjects in which the midshipmen would be required to qualify.

"One of the first and most important requests I have to make," said Whittam presently, "is that none of you touch the switches, except by direction. None of you can guess the harm that might follow the careless and ignorant handling of a switch."

"It's pretty cheeky for an enlisted man to talk to midshipmen about ignorance," whispered Pennington to Farley.

"Oh, I don't know—" Farley started to reply, but Darrin's quiet voice broke in with authority:

"Cease talking in section."

Farley knew this to be a merited rebuke, and accepted it as such, but Pennington's face went violently red.

"Confound that grease–spot–chaser," growled Pen. "He'll be bound to take it out of me as long as the cruise lasts. But I'll get even with him. No cheap greaser is going to ride over me!"

That morning none of the midshipmen were called upon to handle any of the fascinating–looking machinery. Nearly the whole of this tour of practical instruction was taken up by the remarks of the chief electrician. As he spoke, Whittam moved over to one piece or another of mechanism and explained its uses. Finally, he began to question the attentive young men, to see how much of his instruction they had absorbed.

"This is a shame, to set an enlisted man up over us as quiz–master, just to see how little we know," growled Pennington; but this time he had the good sense not to address his remark to anyone.

Pennington was not yet in good shape, after his harrowing experiences of the day before.

Ere the tour of instruction was over, he began to shift somewhat uneasily.

Then his attention began to wander.

A brilliantly shining brass rod near him caught his eye. Something about the glossy metal fascinated him.

Once or twice Pen put out his hand to touch the rod, but as quickly reconsidered and drew back his hand.

At last, however, the temptation proved too strong. He slid one hand along the rail.

"Here, sir, don't handle that!" rasped in the voice of Whittam.

Pennington drew back his hand, a flush mounting to his face.

"The fellow has no right to talk to a midshipman in that fashion!" quivered Pennington to himself. "But it was the fault of that low–minded greaser Darrin, anyway. Darrin saw me, and he glanced swiftly at the chief electrician to draw attention to me."

It is only just to Pennington to state that he actually believed he had seen Dave do this. Darrin, however, was not guilty of the act. He had in no way sought to direct attention at Pennington.

Towards the close of the tour the officer in whose department this instruction fell passed through the dynamo room.

"Are there any breaches of conduct to be reported, Whittam?" inquired the officer, halting.

"Nothing worth mentioning, sir," replied the chief electrician.

"I asked you, Whittam, whether there had been any breaches of conduct," retorted the officer with some asperity.

"One midshipman, sir, after having been instructed to touch nothing, rested his hand on one of the brass rods."

"His name?"

"I don't know the names of many of the young gentlemen yet, sir, so I don't know the particular midshipman's name, sir."

"Then point him out to me," insisted the officer.

There was hardly any need to do so. Pennington's face, flushed with mortification, was sufficient identification. But the chief electrician stepped over, halting in front of the hapless one, and said:

"This is the young gentleman, sir."

"Your name, sir?" demanded the officer.

"Pennington, sir."

"Mr. Pennington, you will place yourself on the report, sir, for disobedience of orders," commanded the officer. "Is this the only case, Whittam?"

"The only case, sir."

The officer passed out of the dynamo room, leaving the unlucky one more than ever angry with Darrin, whom he incorrectly charged with his present trouble.

The recall sounding, Dave turned to Whittam, saying crisply but pleasantly:

"Thank you for our instruction."

"He's thanking the fellow for my new scrape," growled Pennington inwardly.

Dave marched his section back to deck and dismissed it. Dan Dalzell, as section leader in steam instruction, immediately re–formed it.

"You will report in the engine–room, Mr. Dalzell, to Lieutenant–Commander Forman, who is chief engineer of this ship. He will assign you to an instructor."

"Aye, aye, sir," Dan replied, saluting. "Section, right wheel—march!"

Dan already knew where, down in the bowels of the great battleship, to find the engine room.

Reaching that department, Dan halted his section.

"Section all present, sir," reported Dan, saluting a strange officer, who, however, wore the insignia of a lieutenant–commander.

"Your name, sir?" inquired the officer.

"Dalzell, sir."

"Let your section break ranks. Then you may all follow me, and keep your eyes open, for you will go through one or two dark places."

"Aye, aye, sir. Section break ranks."

Lieutenant—Commander Forman led the way, with all the members of the section wondering what was to be the nature of their first day's work in the engineer department.

Descending lower into the ship, the chief engineer led the young middies over a grating, and paused at the head of an iron ladder.

"Pass down in orderly fashion, single file," directed the chief engineer, halting. "When at the foot of this ladder, cross a grating to port side, and then descend a second ladder, which you will find."

All the midshipmen went down the first ladder in silence. Dan, who had preceded the others, crossed the grating and found the second ladder.

Once more these youngsters descended. Pennington, as though by mere accident, succeeded in following Dave Darrin down the ladder.

Just as they were near the bottom Dave felt a foot descend upon his shoulder, almost with a kick, and then rest there with a crushing pressure.

It hurt keenly until Darrin was able to dodge out from under and hurriedly reach the bottom.

"Pardon, whoever you are," came a gruff voice.

Dave, with his shoulder crippled a good deal, and paining keenly, halted as soon as his foot had touched bottom. It was dark down there, though some reflected light came from an incandescent light at a distance.

Dave waited, to peer into the face of the man who had stepped on his shoulder.

It was Pennington, of course!

"I'll take pains not to go down ahead of you again, or to follow you up a ladder," grunted Darrin suspiciously.

27

"Oh, are you the man on whose shoulder my foot rested?" asked Pennington, with apparent curiosity.

"Didn't you know it!" questioned Darrin, looking straight into the other's eyes.

Instead of answering intelligibly, Pennington turned and walked away a few feet.

"Perhaps that fellow thinks he's going to vent his spite on me in a lot of petty ways," murmured Dave. "If that is the idea he has in his head, he's going to wake up one of these days!"

Following the last midshipman came Lieutenant–Commander Forman.

"After me, gentlemen," directed the chief engineer. He turned down a narrow passage, only a few feet long, and came out in the furnace room.

Here huge fires glowed through the furnace doors. Four of the Navy's firemen stood resting on their shovels. Instantly, on perceiving the chief engineer, however, the men stood at attention.

"Pass the word for the chief water tender," ordered the engineer, turning to one of the firemen.

The messenger soon came back with a pleasant–faced, stalwart man of forty.

"Heistand," ordered the chief engineer, "give these members of the first section, third: class, steam instruction, a thorough drill in firing."

"Aye, aye, sir," replied the chief water tender, saluting.

"Heistand's orders are mine, Mr. Dalzell," continued the lieutenant–commander, facing Dan. "Preserve order in your section."

"Aye, aye, sir," replied Dan, saluting. Acknowledging this courtesy in kind, the chief engineer turned and left the furnace room.

Heistand was presumably of German parentage, though he had no accent. He struck the midshipmen as being a pleasant, wholesome fellow, though the water tenders and firemen of the "Massachusetts" knew that he could be extremely strict and grim at need.

"You will now, young gentlemen," began Heistand, "proceed to learn all about priming a furnace, lighting, building, cleaning and generally taking care of a fire. Two furnaces have been left idle for this instruction."

But two of the regular firemen now remained in the room. These were ordered to hustle out coal before boilers B and D. Then Heistand taught the members of the section how to swing a shovel to the best advantage so as to get in a maximum of coal with the least effort. He also illustrated two or three incorrect ways of shoveling coal.

"The idea of making coal heavers out of us!" growled a much-disgusted voice.

Dan did not see who the speaker was, but his eyes flashed as he turned and rasped out:

"Silence in the section! Speak only to ask for information, and then at the proper time."

"Another young autocrat!" muttered a voice.

"Wait one moment, please, Heistand," begged Dan. Then, wheeling squarely about, and facing all the members of the section, he declared with emphasis:

"If there's any more unauthorized talking I shall feel obliged to pass the word above that discipline is in a bad way in this section."

Then he wheeled about once more, facing the chief water tender.

"Now, young gentlemen," resumed the chief water tender, "take your shovels and fill in lively under boilers B and D."

Three or four times Heistand checked one or another of the midshipmen, to show him a more correct way of handling the shovel. Yet, in good time, both furnaces were primed.

"Now, Mr. Dalzell, please detail four members of the section to follow me with their shovels and bring red coals from under another boiler."

Dan appointed himself, Darrin, Farley and Pennington.

Burning coals were brought and thrown into each furnace, and in a little while roaring fires were going. These, though not needed for the handling of the battleship, were permitted to burn for a while, Heistand explaining to the section practically the uses of the water gauges and the test cocks. By this time the midshipmen's white working clothes were liberally sprinkled with coal dust and somewhat smeared with oils.

"And now, young gentlemen, as we have no further use for these fires, you will next learn how to haul them," announced Heistand.

This was interesting work, but hot and fast. The implements with which the middies worked soon became red–hot at the end. Yet, as all entered into this novel work with zest, the fires had soon been hauled out on to the floor plates.

Just as the last of this work was being done Pennington, as an apparent accident due to excess of zeal, dropped the red–hot end of his implement across the toe of Darrin's left shoe.

In an instant the leather began to blaze. With swift presence of mind Dave stepped his right foot on the flame, smothering it at once.

But he was "mad clean through."

"See here, Pen," he muttered, in a low voice, his eyes blazing fiercely into the other midshipman's, "that is the last piece of impudence that will be tolerated from you."

Midshipman Pennington's lip curled disdainfully.

Dan had not seen the "accident," but he was near enough to hear the talking, and he caught Dave at it. So Dan ordered, impartially:

"Mr. Darrin, you will place yourself on report for unauthorized talking in section!"

Dave flushed still more hotly, but said nothing.

Midshipman Dalzell now marched the section from the furnace room, and dismissed it. It was near noon, and would soon be time for the middies to eat.

Dave hurried away, washed, changed his uniform, and then stepped away swiftly to place himself on the report.

"I was sorry to do that, old chum," murmured Dan, as he met Dave returning. "But of course I couldn't play favorites. What made you so far forget yourself?"

"A something that would have had the same effect on you," retorted Dave grimly. Thereupon he described Pennington's two underhanded assaults that morning.

"Humph!" muttered Dalzell. "That fellow Pen is bound to go the whole limit with you."

"He won't go much further," declared Dave, his eyes flashing.

"And the chump ought to know it, too," mused Dan. "The class history of the last year should have taught him that. But see here, Dave, I don't believe Pen will do anything openly. He will construct a series of plausible accidents."

"There will be one thing about him that will be open, if he goes any further," retorted Dave, "and that will be his face when he collides with my fist."

"I hope I see that when it happens," grinned Dalzell. "It's bound to be entertaining!"

"Wait a second, then. Here comes Pennington now," murmured Dave Darrin in an undertone.

Pennington, in his immaculate blue uniform, like the chums, came strolling along the passageway between decks.

He affected not to see the chums, and would have passed by. But Dave, eyeing him closely, waited until Pen was barely three feet away. Then Darrin said tersely:

"Mr. Pennington, I wish an understanding with you."

"I don't want any with you," replied Pennington insolently, as he stared at Dave from under much-raised eyebrows. He would have gone by, but Dave sprang squarely in front of him.

"Just wait a moment!" warned Dave rather imperiously, for he was aglow with justifiable indignation.

"Well?" demanded Pennington halting. "Out with it, whatever you may think you have to say."

"I have two things to speak about," replied Dave, trying to control his voice. "In the first place, while going down the ladders to the furnaces this morning, you stepped on my shoulder."

"Well!" insisted Pennington coldly.

"The second thing you did was, when hauling the fires, to drop red-hot metal across one of my shoes, setting it on fire."

"Well?" insisted Pennington more coldly.

"If you mean to contend that either one was an accident," resumed Dave, "then—"

But he found himself obliged to pause for a moment in order to steady his voice.

"Well?" asked Pennington with more insolence than ever.

"If you make such pretense in either case," tittered Dave Darrin, "then you're a liar!"

"Fellow!" sputtered Pennington, turning white with anger.

"I mean what I say, and I can back it up," muttered Darrin.

"Then I'll make you eat your words!" roared Pennington.

Clenching his fists and with the boxer's attitude, Pen aimed two swift blows at Darrin.

Neither blow reached, however, for Dave dodged out of the way. Then Darrin struck back, a straight, true, forceful blow that landed on the other midshipman's nose, knocking him down.

Pennington staggered somewhat when he rose, but he was quickly up, none the less, and ready for anything that might happen.

All of a sudden Dan Dalzell felt his own heart going down into his shoes. One of the ship's officers had just entered the passageway, in time to see what was going on.

CHAPTER IV. A LITTLE MEETING ASHORE

"Stop it, both of you," whispered Dan.

"Stand at attention, ready to salute the officer."

Pennington, with the blood flowing from his damaged nose, would have made a most ludicrous figure saluting!

The instant that he saw such evidence as Pen's nose presented the officer would be bound to make inquiries.

Then, just as surely, his next step must be to Border the three before the commandant of midshipmen.

Fighting carries with it a severe penalty. Even Dan was certain to be reported, through the mere fact of his presence there, as aiding in a fight. And those who aid are punished as severely as the principals themselves.

It was a tense, fearsome instant, for midshipmen have been dismissed from the Naval Academy for this very offense.

The passage was not brilliantly lighted.

The on−coming officer, a lieutenant, junior grade, was looking at the floor as he came along.

Suddenly he paused, seemed lost in thought, then wheeled and walked back whence he had come.

Dan breathed more easily. Dave heaved a sigh of relief.

As for Pennington, that midshipman had wheeled and was stealing rapidly down the passageway, intent only on escape.

"That was the closest squeak we'll ever have without being ragged cold," murmured Dalzell tremulously.

"Where is Pennington?" demanded Dave, wheeling about after he had watched the Naval lieutenant out of sight.

"Ducked out of sight, like a submarine," chuckled Dan.

At that moment the call for midshipmen's dinner formation sounded. Dave and Dan were ready.

Pennington showed up just after the line had started to march into the midshipmen's mess tables.

To the inquiry of the officer in charge, Pen lamely explained that he had bumped his nose into something hard in a poorly lighted passageway.

Though the officer accepted the excuse, he smiled within himself.

"It wasn't iron or steel that bumped that young man's nose," thought the officer.

"Oh, the middies haven't changed a lot since I boned at Annapolis!"

Pennington's nose was no very lovely member of his face at that moment. It had been struck hard, mashed rather flat, and now looked like a red bulb.

"Meet with an accident, Pen?" asked Hallam curiously at table.

"Quit your kidding, please," requested Pennington sulkily.

That directed the curious glances of other middies at Pennington's new bulbous nose.

The young man was so brusque about it, however, that other table mates ceased quizzing him.

Yet, as soon as the meal was over, many a youngster asked others of his class for news regarding Pen. But none possessed it.

During the brief rest that followed the meal, however, Midshipman Pennington made it his business to try to meet Dave Darrin alone. He succeeded, finding Dave staring off across the water at the port rail.

"Of course, Mr. Darrin," began the other midshipman, in a voice suggestive of ice, "you are aware that the incident of an hour ago cannot be allowed to pass unnoticed."

"I don't believe there's any danger of that," retorted Darrin, with an ironical glance at Pennington's damaged–looking nose.

"Confound you, sir," hissed the other midshipman, "don't you dare to be insolent with me."

"Why, I had thought," observed Dave, "that, of your own choice, the period of courtesies between us had passed."

"I shall call you out, Mr. Darrin!"

"You'll find my hearing excellent," smiled Dave. "I shall make but one stipulation."

"I'll do you the favor of asking what that stipulation is," sneered Pennington.

"Why, after the narrow escape we had from being caught and reported, an hour or so ago, I shall ask that the fight be held where we are not so likely to be caught at it. I don't care about being dropped from the Naval Academy, nor do I believe you do."

"It would be a good thing for the service, if one of us were to be dropped," sneered Pennington.

"Yes! Oh, well, you can easily procure writing materials from the captain's clerk," volunteered Dave generously. "On a cruise, I believe, a resignation is sent direct to the commandant of midshipmen."

This ridicule served only to fan the flame of Pennington's wrath.

"Darrin," he hissed, "the Academy isn't big enough to hold us both!"

"But I've already told you how to get out," protested Dave coolly.

"I don't intend to get out!"

"No more do I," rejoined Dave. "I won't even toss pennies with you to find out who quits the service."

"Mr. Darrin, you are merely seeking to divert my mind from what I have said."

"What did you say—particularly?"

"That you would have to fight me."

"I have already signified my entire willingness, Mr. Pennington. To that I really can add nothing."

Fourth classmen are always addressed as "mister," and they must use the same "handle to the name" when addressing upper classmen. But members of the three upper classes resort to the use of "mister," in addressing classmates, only when they wish to be offensive or nearly so.

"I will send a friend to meet you," Pennington continued.

"Why, I thought," bantered Darrin ironically, "that you were going to fight me yourself."

"So I am—be sure of it. I will amend my statement by saying that I will send a second to see you."

"Save time by sending him to Dalzell."

"Very good, Mr. Darrin."

"Is that all you wished to say to me?"

"Yes."

"Very good, Mr. Pennington."

With two very stiff nods the midshipmen parted.

Pennington hastened at once in search of Hallam.

"Will you serve me, old man?" queried Pennington.

"Sorry, but——"

"Well, you see, Pen, not knowing all the facts of the case, I must admit that all my sympathies are with Darrin."

"All your sympathies?" echoed Pen, frowning.

"Well, nearly all, anyway. You see, I've known and observed Darrin for a full year now, and I don't believe patient old Darry is the one to start any trouble."

"He called me a liar," protested Pennington.

"Did he?" gasped Hallam.

"Well, he qualified the statement, but his way of saying it was as offensive as the direct lie could have been."

"So you're bent on fighting Darry?"

"I am."

"Too bad!" muttered Hallam, shaking his head.

"Are you anxious for your idol?" asked Pen in a disagreeable tone.

"No, Penny; it's you that I'm concerned about in my own mind. You're going next to a very hard proposition. Darry is patient—almost as patient as the proverbial camel—but when he fights he fights! You'll be hammered to a pulp, Pen."

"Pooh!"

"No one has yet beaten Darrin at a fist fight."

"There always has to be a first time, you know."

"And you think you're It?"

"As far as Darrin is concerned—yes."

"Too bad—too bad!" sighed Hallam. "I'm afraid, Penny, that the heat in the furnace room was too much for you this morning."

"Then you won't serve as one of my seconds?"

"The honor is most regretfully declined," replied Hallam in a tone of mock sadness.

"You want to see Darrin win?"

"If there has to be a fight, I do," replied Midshipman Hallam.

"Don't bet your money on him, anyway."

"I'm not a gambler, Penny, and I don't bet," replied Hallam, with a dignity that, somehow, ended the conversation.

Pennington had considerable difficulty, at first, in finding a second. At last, however, he induced Decker and Briggs to represent him.

These two midshipmen went to see Dan Dalzell.

"Wait until I send for Mr. Farley," proposed Dalzell. He soon had that midshipman, who was wholly willing to serve Darrin in any capacity.

"We're ready to have the fight this evening," proposed Midshipman Decker.

"We're not," retorted Dan, with vigor.

"Why not?"

"This forenoon Pennington deliberately stepped on Darrin's shoulder, with such force as to lame it a good deal," replied Dan. "Our man insists that he has a right to rest his shoulder, and to wait until to-morrow."

"But to-morrow we have a short shore liberty at Hampton Roads," remonstrated Briggs.

"Yes; and during that shore liberty we can have the fight more safely than on board ship," insisted Dalzell.

"But we intended to devote our shore leave to pleasure," objected Decker.

"You'll find plenty of pleasure, if you accept our proposition," urged Dan dryly. "At any rate, we won't hear of Darrin fighting before to-morrow. He must have to-night to rest that shoulder."

"All right; so be it," growled Decker, after a side glance at Briggs.

"On shore, at some point to be selected by the seconds?" asked Dan Dalzell.

"Yes; that's agreed."

Details as to whom to invite as referee and time–keeper were also arranged.

"I suppose we'll have to use up our shore leave that way, then," grunted Pennington, when told of the arrangement.

"There's one way you can save the day," grinned Decker.

"How?"

"Put Darrin to sleep in the first round, then hurriedly dress and leave, and enjoy your time on shore."

"But Darrin is a very able man with his fists," observed Pennington.

"Yes; but you're a mile bigger and heavier, and you're spry, too. You ought to handle him with all the ease in the world."

"I don't know," muttered Pennington, who didn't intend to make the mistake of bragging in advance. "I'll do my best, of course."

"Oh, you'll win out, if you're awake," predicted Midshipman Briggs confidently.

When the cadets were called, the following morning, they found the battleship fleet at anchor in Hampton Roads.

CHAPTER V. WHEN THE SECONDS WONDERED

One after another the launches sped ashore, carrying their swarms of distinguished looking young midshipmen.

The fight party managed to get off all in the same boat, and on one of the earliest trips.

Pennington was to have ordinary shore leave on the cruise, his fifty demerits to be paid for by loss of privileges on his return to the Naval Academy.

"Decker," proposed Dan, "you and I can skip away and find a good place in no time. Then we can come back after the others."

"That's agreeable to me," nodded Midshipman Decker.

In twenty minutes the two seconds were back.

"We've found just the place," announced Decker. "And it isn't more than three minutes' walk from here. Will you all hurry along?"

"The place" turned out to be a barn that had not been used for a year or more. The floor was almost immaculately clean. In consideration of two dollars handed him, the owner had agreed to display no curiosity, and not to mention the affair to any one.

"How do you like it, Darry?" asked Dan anxiously.

"It will suit me as well as any other place," responded Dave, slipping off his blouse, folding it neatly and putting it aside, his uniform cap following.

"And you?" asked Decker of his man.

"The floor's hard, but I don't expect to be the man to hit it," replied Pennington.

In five minutes both midshipmen were attired for their "affair." Between them the different members of the party had smuggled ashore shoes, old trousers and belts for the fighters.

It being a class affair, Remington, of the third class, had come along as referee, while Dawley; was to be the time–keeper.

"If the principals are ready, let them step forward," ordered Midshipman Remington, going to the middle of the floor. "Now, I understand that this is to be a finish fight; rounds, two minutes; rests, two minutes. I also understand that the principals do not care to shake hands before the call to mix up."

Darrin and Pennington nodded their assent.

"Take your places, gentlemen," ordered the referee quickly. "Are you ready, gentlemen?"

"Yes," came from both principals.

"Time!"

Both men had their guards up. As the word left the referee's lips each tried two or three passes which the other blocked. Midshipman Pennington was trying to take his opponent's "measure."

Then Dave ducked, darted, dodged and wheeled about. Pennington had to follow him, and it made the latter angry.

"Stand up and fight, can't you," hissed Pen.

"Silence during the rounds, Mr. Pennington," admonished the referee quietly. "Let the officials do all the talking that may be necessary."

Dave, as he dodged again, and came up unscathed, grinned broadly over this rebuke. That grin made Pen angrier than anything else could have done.

"I'll wipe that grin off his face!" muttered Pennington angrily.

And this very thing Pennington tried hard to do. He was quick on his own feet, and for a few seconds he followed the dodging Darrin about, raining in blows that required all of Dave's adroitness to escape.

Dave's very success, however, made his opponent all the angrier. From annoyance, followed by excessive irritation, Pennington went into almost blind rage—and the man who does that, anywhere in life, must always pay for it.

Suddenly Dave swung his right in on the point of Pen's chin with a force that jolted the larger midshipman. As part of the same movement, Darrin's left crashed against Pennington's nose.

Then, out of chivalry, Dave dropped back, to give Pen a few moments, in case he needed them, to get his wits back.

"Time!" roared Dawley, and Pennington's seconds pounced upon him and bore him away to his corner.

"Now I know how that fellow Darrin wins his fights," growled Pennington in an undertone. "He keeps on running away until he has the other man gasping for breath. Then Darrin jumps in and wins."

"The method doesn't much matter," commented Briggs dryly, as he and Decker worked over their man. "It's the result that counts. Rush Darry into a tight corner, Pen, and then slam him hard and sufficiently."

"Thanks, fellows; now I'm all right for the second round." muttered Midshipman Pennington.

In a few seconds more Dave and his opponent were hard at work.

Dave still used his footwork, and most cleverly. Yet, wherever he went, Pen followed him nimbly. It didn't look so one sided now.

Then Pennington, at last, managed to deliver one blow on Darrin's right short ribs. It took a lot of Dave's spare wind; he raced about, seeking to regain his wind before allowing close quarters. But at last Pennington closed in again, and, after a swift feint, tried to land the same short–rib blow.

Darrin was watching, and blocked. Then, his temples reddening with anger, Dave swung in a huge one that crashed in under Pennington's right ear.

"Time!" shouted Dawley, just as Pen went to the floor in a heap. That saved the larger midshipman from having to take the count. His seconds had him ready at the call for the third round.

Now, suddenly, Darrin seemed to change not only his tactics, but his whole personality. To his opponent Dave seemed suddenly transformed into a dancing demon.

It was about the same old footwork, but it was aggressive now, instead of being defensive.

First, Dave landed a light tap on the already suffering nose. A few seconds later he landed on the point of Pen's chin, though not hard enough to send his man down. Then a rather light blow on the jaw, just under Pen's right ear again. The larger midshipman was now thoroughly alarmed. He feared that Darrin could do whatever he willed, and shivered with wonder as to when the knockout blow would come.

The truth was, Pennington was still putting up a better battle than he himself realized, and Darrin was not disposed to take any foolish chances through rushing the affair. Thus, the third round ended.

By the time that they came up for the fourth round, after both men had undergone some vigorous handling by their respective seconds, Pennington was a good deal revived and far more confident.

Dave's tactics were the same in the fourth round. Pennington didn't find time to develop much in the way of tactics for himself, save to defend himself.

During the first minute no important blows were landed on either side. Then, suddenly, Dave darted in and under, and brought a right−arm hook against Pen's nose in a way that started that member to bleeding again, and with a steady flow.

That jarred the larger midshipman. He plunged in, heavily and blindly, blocking one of Darrin's blows by wrapping both arms around him.

"None of that, Mr. Pennington! Break away fast!" ordered Midshipman Remington quickly.

Dave took a fair get away, not attempting to strike as the clinch was broken. But an instant later Dave came back, dancing all around his dazed opponent, landing on the short ribs, on the breast bone, under either ear and finally on the tip of the chin.

Pen was sure that none of these blows had been delivered with the force that Darrin could have sent in.

"Time!" shouted Midshipman Dawley.

The principals retired to their corners, Pennington almost wholly afraid from the conviction that his antagonist was now merely playing with him to keep the interest going.

So Pennington was still rather badly scared when the two came together for the fifth round.

"Get lively, now, gentlemen, if you can," begged Referee Remington. "Finish this one way or the other, and let us get some of the benefits of our shore leave."

Pen started by putting more steam behind every blow. Dave, who had used up so much of his wind by his brilliant footwork, began to find it harder to keep the upper hand.

Twice, however, he managed to land body blows. He was trying to drive in a third when Pennington blocked, following this with a left–arm jab on Darrin's left jaw that sent the lighter man to the floor.

Instantly Dawley began to count off the seconds.

"—seven, eight, nine, te——"

Dave was up on his feet. Pen tried to make a quick rush, but Darrin dodged cleverly, them wheeled and faced his opponent as the latter wheeled about.

After that there was less footwork. Both men stood up to it, as keenly alert as they could be, each trying to drive home heavy blows. While they were still at it the call of time sounded.

"Don't let him put it over you, David, little giant!" warned Dan, as the latter and Farley vigorously massaged Darrin's muscles. "He all but had you, and there isn't any need of making Pen a present of the meeting."

"I tried to get him," muttered Dave in an undertone, "and I shall go on trying to the last. But Pennington is pretty nearly superior to anyone in my class."

"Just waltz in and show him," whispered Dalzell, as the call sounded.

Pennington entered the sixth round with more confidence. He began, at the outset, to drive in heavy blows, nor did Dave do much dodging.

Bump! Twenty–five seconds only of this round had gone when Darrin landed his right fist with fearful force upon the high point of Pennington's jaw.

Down went the larger midshipman again. This time he moaned. His eyes were open, though they had a somewhat glassy look in them.

Dawley was counting off the seconds in measured tones.

"—seven, eight, nine—ten!"

Pen had struggled to rise to his feet, but sank back with a gasp of despair and rage.

"Mr. Pennington loses the count and the fight," announced Referee Remington coolly. "I don't believe we're needed here, Dawley. The seconds can handle the wreck. Come along."

As the two officials of the meeting hustled out of the barn, Dalzell gave his attention to helping his chum, while Farley went over to offer his services in getting the vanquished midshipman into shape.

"There were times when I could have closed both of Pennington's eyes," murmured Dave to Dan. "But I didn't want to give him any disfiguring marks that would start questions on board ship."

"You had him whipped from the start," murmured Dan confidently, as he sprayed, then rubbed Dave's chest and arms.

"Maybe, but I'm not so sure of that," rejoined Darrin. "That fellow isn't so easy a prize for any one in my class. There were times when I was all but convinced that he had me."

"Oh, fairy tales!" grunted Dan.

"Have it your own way, then, Danny boy!"

When Darrin and his seconds left the barn they went off to enjoy what remained of the shore leave. Pennington's seconds finally, at his own request, left him at an ice cream parlor, where he proposed to remain until he could return to the big, steel "Massachusetts" without exciting any wonder over the little time he had remained ashore. Pennington had strength to walk about, but he was far from being in really good shape, and preferred to keep quiet.

CHAPTER VI. IN TROUBLE ON FOREIGN SOIL

From Hampton Roads the Battleship Squadron, with the midshipmen on board, sailed directly for Plymouth, England.

During most of the voyage over slow cruising speed was used. By the time that England's coast was sighted the third–class middies found they knew much more about a battleship than they had believed to be possible at the start of the voyage.

They had served as firemen; they had mastered many of the electrical details of a battleship; they had received instruction and had "stood trick" by the engines; there had been some drill with the smaller, rapid–fire guns, and finally, they had learned at least the rudiments of "wig–wagging," as signaling by means of signal flags is termed.

It was just before the call to supper formation when England's coast loomed up. Most of the midshipmen stood at the rail, watching eagerly for a better glimpse at the coast.

Some of the midshipmen, especially those who came from wealthier families, had been in

England before entering the Naval Academy. These fortunate ones were questioned eagerly by their comrades.

The battleships were well in sight of Eastern King Point when the midshipmen's call for supper formation sounded. Feeling that they would much have preferred to wait for their supper, the young men hastened below.

After the line was formed it seemed to the impatient young men as though it had never taken so long to read the orders.

Yet there came one welcome order, to the effect that, immediately after the morning meal, all midshipmen might go to the pay officer and draw ten dollars, to be charged against their pay accounts.

"That ten dollars apiece looms up large David, little giant," murmured Dan Dalzell, while the evening meal was in progress.

"We ought to have a lot of fun on it," replied Darrin, who was looking forward with greatest eagerness to his first visit to any foreign soil. "But how much shore leave are we to have?"

"Two days, the word is. We'll get it straight in the morning, at breakfast formation."

In defiance of regulations, Midshipman Pennington, whose father was wealthy, had several hundred dollars concealed in his baggage. He had already invited Hallam, Mossworth and Dickey to keep in his wake on shore, and these young men had gladly enough agreed.

"Say, but we're slackening speed!" quivered Dalzell, when the meal was nearly finished.

"Headway has stopped," declared Darrin a few moments later.

"Listen, everyone!" called Farley. "Don't you hear the rattle of the anchor chains?"

"Gentlemen, as we're forbidden to make too much racket," proposed irrepressible Dan, "let us give three silent cheers for Old England!"

Rising in his place, Dan raised his hand aloft, and brought it down, as his lips silently formed a "hurrah!"

Three times this was done, each time the lips of the midshipmen forming a silent cheer.

Then Dan, with a mighty swoop of his right arm, let his lips form the word that everyone knew to be "tiger!"

"Ugh-h-h!" groaned Midshipman Reilly.

"Throw that irresponsible Fenian out!" directed Dan, grinning.

Then the midshipmen turned their attention to the remnants of the meal.

Boom! sounded sharply overhead.

"There goes the twenty-one-gunner," announced Darrin.

When a foreign battleship enters a fortified port the visiting fleet, or rather, its flagship, fires a national salute of twenty-one guns. After a short interval following the discharge of the last gun, one of the forts on shore answers with twenty-one guns. This is one of the methods of observing the courtesies between nations by their respective fleets.

Ere all the guns had been fired from the flagship, the third classmen received the rising signal; the class marched out and was dismissed. Instantly a break was made for deck.

The midshipmen were in good time to see the smoke and hear the roar of guns from one of the forts on shore.

In the morning the commandant of cadets, as commanding officer of the squadron, would go ashore with his aide and pay a formal call to the senior military officer. Later in the day that English officer and one or two of his staff officers would return the call by coming out to the flagship. That accomplished, all the required courtesies would have been observed.

It was still broad daylight, for in summer the English twilight is a long one, and darkness does not settle down until late.

"Oh, if we were only going ashore to-night!" murmured Hallam. There were many others to echo the thought, but all knew that it could not be done.

"Couldn't we find a trick for slipping ashore after lights out?" eagerly queried Dickey, who was not noted as a "greaser."

"Could we?" quivered Hallam, who, with few demerits against him, felt inclined to take a chance.

But Pennington, to whom he appealed, shook his head.

"Too big a risk, Hally," replied Pen. "And trebly dangerous, with that greaser, Darrin, in the class."

"Oh, stow that," growled Hallam. "Darrin is no greaser. You've got him on your black books—that's all."

"He is a greaser, I tell you," cried Pennington fiercely.

There were a score of midshipmen in this group, and many of them nodded approvingly at Pennington's statement. Though still a class leader, Dave had lost some of his popularity since his report to the police of Annapolis.

So the middies turned in, that night, with unsatisfied dreams of shore life in England.

Soon after breakfast the next morning, however, every midshipman had drawn his ten dollars, even to Pennington, who had no use for such a trifling amount.

As fast as possible the launches ranged alongside at the side gangway, taking off groups of midshipmen, everyone of whom had been cautioned to be at dock in time to board a launch in season for supper formation.

Pennington and his party were among the first to land. They hurried away.

Dave Darrin's Second Year at Annapolis

It was on the second trip of one of the launches that Dave, Dan and Farley made their get away. These three chums had agreed to stick together during the day. They landed at the Great Western Docks, to find themselves surrounded by eager British cabbies.

"Are we going to take a cab and get more quickly and intelligently to the best part of the town to see?" asked Farley.

"I don't vote for it," replied Darrin. "We have only five dollars apiece for each of the two days we're to be ashore. I move that we put in the forenoon, anyway, in prowling about the town for ourselves. We'll learn more than we would by riding."

"Come on, then," approved Dan.

Plymouth is an old—fashioned English seaport that has been rather famous ever since the thirteenth century. Many parts of the town, including whole streets, look as though the houses had been built since that time. This is especially true of many of the streets near the water front.

For two hours the three middies roamed through the streets, often meeting fellow classmen. Wherever the young midshipmen went many of the English workmen and shopkeepers raised their hats in friendly salute of the American uniform.

"We don't seem to run across Pen's gang anywhere," remarked Farley at last.

"Oh, no," smiled Dave. "That's a capitalistic crowd. They'll hit only the high spots."

Nevertheless, these three poor—in—purse midshipmen enjoyed themselves hugely in seeing the quaint old town. At noon they found a real old English chop house, where they enjoyed a famous meal.

"I wish we could slip some of these little mutton pies back with us!" sighed Dan wistfully.

In the afternoon the three chums saw the newer market place, where all three bought small souvenirs for their mothers at home. Darrin also secured a little remembrance present for his sweetheart, Belle Meade.

The guild hall and some of the other famous buildings were visited.

Later in the afternoon Dave began to inspect his watch every two or three minutes.

"No need for us to worry, with Dave's eye glued to his watch," laughed Dan.

"Come on, fellows," summoned Darrin finally. "We haven't more than time now to make the dock and get back to supper formation."

"Take a cab?" asked Farley. "You know, we've found that they're vastly cheaper than American cabs."

"No-o-o, not for me," decided Dave. "We'll need the rest of our shore money to-morrow, and our legs are good and sturdy."

Yet even careful Dave, as it turned out, had allowed no more than time. The chums reached the dock in time to see the launches half way between the fleet and shore. Some forty other midshipmen stood waiting on the dock.

Among these were Pennington and his party, all looking highly satisfied with their day's sport, as indeed they were.

Pennington's eyes gleamed when he caught sight of Darrin, Dalzell and Farley—for Pen had a scheme of his own in mind.

Not far from Pennington stood a little Englishman with keen eyes and a jovial face. Pen stepped over to him.

"There are the three midshipmen I was telling you about," whispered Pennington, slipping a half sovereign into the Englishman's hand. "You thoroughly understand your part in the joke, don't you?"

"Don't h'I, though—just, sir!" laughed the undersized Englishman, and strolled away.

Darrin and his friends were soon informed by classmates that the launches now making shore-ward were coming in on their last trip for midshipmen.

"Well, we're here in plenty of time," sighed Dave contentedly.

"Oh, I knew we'd be, with you holding the watch," laughed Dan in his satisfied way.

As the three stood apart they were joined by the undersized Englishman, who touched his hat to them with a show of great respect.

"Young gentlemen," he inquired, "h'I suppose, h'of course, you've 'ad a look h'at the anchor h'of Sir Francis Drake's flagship, the time 'e went h'out h'and sank the great Spanish h'Armada?"

"Why, no, my friend," replied Dave, looking at the man with interest. "Is that here at Plymouth?"

"H'assuredly, sir. H'and h'only a minute's walk h'over to that shed yonder, sir. H'if you'll come with me, young gentlemen, h'I'll show h'it to you. H'it's one of h'our biggest sights, h'and it's in me own custody, at present. Come this way, young gentlemen."

"That sounds like something worth seeing," declared Dave to his comrades. "Come along. It'll take the launches at least six minutes to get in, and then they'll stay tied up here for another five minutes."

With only a single backward glance at the young midshipmen, the undersized Englishman was already leading the way.

At quickened pace the young midshipmen reached the shed that had been indicated. Their guide had already drawn a key from a pocket, and had unsnapped the heavy padlock.

"Step right in, young gentlemen, h'and h'I'll follow h'and show h'it to you."

Unsuspecting, the three middies stepped inside the darkened shed. Suddenly the door banged, and a padlock clicked outside.

"Here, stop that, you rascally joker!" roared Dalzell, wheeling about. "What does this mean?"

"Big trouble!" spoke Dave Darrin seriously and with a face from which the color was fast receding.

CHAPTER VII. PENNINGTON GETS HIS WISH

"The scoundrel!" gasped Farley, his face whiter than any of the others.

Dave was already at the door, trying to force it open. But he might almost as well have tried to lift one of the twelve–inch guns of the battleship "Massachusetts."

"We're locked in—that's sure!" gasped Dalzell, almost dazed by the catastrophe.

"And what's more, we won't get out in a hurry, unless we can make some of our classmates hear," declared Dave.

For the next half minute they yelled themselves nearly hoarse, but no response came.

"What could have been that little cockney's purpose in playing this shabby trick on us?" demanded Farley.

"Perhaps the cockney thinks we're admirals, with our pockets lined with gold. Perhaps he and some of his pals intend to rob us, later in the evening," proposed Dan, with a ghastly grin.

"Any gang would find something of a fight on their hands, then," muttered Dave Darrin grimly.

All three were equally at a loss to think of any explanation for such a "joke" as this. Equally improbable did it seem that any thugs of the town would expect to reap any harvest from robbing three midshipmen.

Desperately they turned to survey their surroundings. The shed was an old one, yet strongly built. There were no windows, no other door save that at which the three middies now stood baffled.

"Another good old yell," proposed Darrin.

It was given with a lusty will, but proved as fruitless as the former one.

"We don't take the last launch back to ship," declared Farley, wild with rage.

"Which means a long string of demerits," said Dan.

"No shore leave to–morrow, either," groaned Darrin. "Fellows, this mishap will affect our shore leave throughout all the cruise."

"We can explain it," suggested Farley with a hopefulness that he did not feel at all.

"Of course we can," jeered Dave Darrin. "But what officer is fool enough to believe such a cock–and–bull story as this one will seem? At the very least, the commandant would believe that we had been playing some pretty stiff prank ourselves, in order to get treated in this fashion. No, no, fellows! We may just as well undeceive ourselves, and prepare to take the full soaking of discipline that we're bound to get. If we attempted this sort of explanation, we'd be lucky indeed to get through the affair without being tried by general court–martial for lying."

"Drake's anchor, indeed!" exclaimed Dan in deep self disgust.

"We ought to have known better," grunted Farley, equally enraged with himself. "What on earth made us so absent–minded as to believe that a priceless relic would be kept in an old shed like this?"

"We're sure enough idiots!" groaned Dan.

"Hold on there, fellows," interrupted Dave Darrin. "Vent all your anger right on me. I'm the great and only cause of this misfortune. It was I who proposed that we take up that cockney's invitation. I'm the real and only offender against decent good sense, and yet you both have to suffer with me."

"Let's give another yell, bigger than before," suggested Dan weakly.

They did, but with no better result than before.

"The launches are away now, anyway, I guess," groaned Farley, after consulting his watch.

"Yes, and we're up the tree with the commandant," grunted Dalzell bitterly.

"Yell again?" asked Farley.

"No," retorted Dave, shaking his head. "We've seen the uselessness of asking help from outside. Let's supply our own help. Now, then—altogether! Shoulder the door!"

A savage assault they hurled upon the door. But they merely caused it to vibrate.

"We can't do it," gasped Dan, after the third trial.

Considerable daylight filtered in through the cracks at top, bottom and one side of the door. Further back in the shed there was less light.

"Let's explore this old place in search of hope," begged Dave.

Together they started back, looking about keenly in what appeared to be an empty room.

"Say! Look at that!" cried Dave suddenly.

He pointed to a solid looking, not very heavy ship's spar.

"What good will that thing do us?" asked Farley rather dubiously.

"Let's see if we can raise it to our shoulders," proposed Dave Darrin radiantly. "Then well find out!"

"Hurrah!" quivered Dan Dalzell, bending over the spar at the middle.

"Up with it!" commanded Darrin, placing himself at the head of the spar. Farley took hold at the further end.

Dave Darrin's Second Year at Annapolis

"Up with it!" heaved Midshipman Darrin.

Right up the spar went. It would have been a heavy job for three young men of their size in civil life, but midshipmen are constantly undergoing the best sort of physical training.

"Now, then—a fast run and a hard bump!" called Darrin.

At the door they rushed, bearing the spar as a battering ram.

Bump! The door shook and shivered.

"Once more may do it!" cheered Darrin. "Back."

Again they dashed the head of their battering ram against the door. It gave way, and, climbing through, they raced back to the pier.

But Dan, who had secured the lead, stopped with a groan, pointing out over the water.

"Not a bit of good, fellows! There go the launches, and we're the only fellows left! It's all up with our summer's fun!"

"Is it, though?" shouted Dave, spurting ahead. "Come on and find out!"

As they reached the front of the piers, down at the edge of a landing stage they espied a little steam tender.

"That boat has to take us out to the 'Massachusetts'!" cried Darrin desperately, as he plunged down the steps to the landing stage, followed by his two chums.

[Illustration: The Three Midshipmen Raced Toward the Pier.]

"Who's the captain here?" called Dave, racing across the landing stage to the tender's gangplank.

"I am, sir," replied a portly, red-faced Englishman, leaning out of the wheel-house window.

"What'll you charge to land us in haste aboard the American battleship 'Massachusetts'?" asked Darrin eagerly.

"Half a sov. will be about right, sir," replied the tender's skipper, touching his cap at sight of the American Naval uniform.

"Good enough," glowed Dave, leaping aboard. "Cast off as quickly as you can, captain, or we'll be in a heap of trouble with our discipline officers."

The English skipper was quick to act. He routed out two deckhands, who quickly cast off. Almost while the deckhands were doing this the skipper rang the engineer's bell.

"Come into the wheel–'ouse with me," invited the skipper pleasantly, which invitation the three middies accepted. "Now, then, young gentlemen, 'ow did it 'appen that you missed your own launches."

"It was a mean trick—a scoundrelly one!" cried Darrin resentfully. Then he described just what had happened.

The skipper's own bronzed cheeks burned to a deeper color.

"I can 'ardly believe that an Englishman would play such a trick on young h'officers of a friendly power," he declared. "But I told you, sir, the fare out to your ship would be half a sov. I lied. If a nasty little cockney played such a trick on you, it's my place, as a decent Englishman, to take you out for nothing—and that's the fare."

"Oh, we'll gladly pay the half sov." protested Darrin.

"Not on this craft you can't, sir," replied the skipper firmly.

Looking eagerly ahead, the three middies saw two of the launches go along side of the "Massachusetts" and discharge passengers. As the second left the side gangway the Briton, who had been crowding on steam well, ranged in along side.

"What craft is that, and what do you want?" hailed the officer of the deck, from above.

"The tender 'Lurline,' sir, with three of your gentlemen to put h'aboard of you, sir," the Briton bellowed through a window of the wheel–house.

"Very good, then. Come alongside," directed the officer of the deck.

In his most seamanlike style the Briton ranged alongside. Dave tried to press the fare upon the skipper, but he would have none of that. So the three shook hands swiftly but heartily with him, then sprang across to the side gangway, where they paused long enough to lift their caps to this stranger and friend. The Briton lifted his own cap, waving it heartily, ere he fell off and turned about.

"You didn't get aboard any too soon, gentlemen," remarked the officer of the deck, eyeing the three middies keenly as they came up over the side, doffing their uniform caps to the colors. "Hustle for the formation."

Midshipman Pennington was chuckling deeply over the supposed fact that he had at last succeeded in bringing Darrin in for as many demerits as Darrin had helped heap upon him.

"That'll break his heart as an avowed greaser," Pen told himself. "With all the demerits Darrin will get, he'll have no heart for greasing the rest of this year. It's rough on Farley, but I'm not quite as sorry for Dalzell, who, in his way, is almost as bad as Darrin. He's Darrin's cuckoo and shadow, anyway. Oh, I wish I could see Darrin's face now!"

This last was uttered just as Midshipman Pennington stepped into line at the supper formation.

"I wish I could see Darrin's face now!" Pen repeated to himself.

Seldom has a wish been more quickly gratified. For, just in the nick of time to avoid being reported, Midshipmen Darrin, Dalzell and Farley came into sight, falling into their respective places.

At that instant it was Midshipman Pennington's face, not Dave Darrin's, that was really worth studying.

"Now how did the shameless greaser work this!" Pennington pondered uneasily.

But, of course, he couldn't ask. He could only hope that, presently, he would hear the whole story from some other man in the class.

CHAPTER VIII. THE TRAGEDY OF THE GALE

There is altogether too much to the summer practice cruise for it to be related in detail.

Nor would the telling of it prove interesting to the reader. When at sea, save on Sundays, the midshipman's day is one of hard toil.

It is no life for the indolent young man. He is routed out early in the morning and put at hard work.

On a midshipman's first summer cruise what he learns is largely the work that is done by the seamen, stokers, water tenders, electricians, the signal men and others.

Yet he must learn every phase of all this work thoroughly, for some day, before he becomes an officer, he must be examined as to his knowledge of all this great mass of detail.

It is only when in port that some relaxation comes into the midshipman's life. He has shore leave, and a large measure of liberty. Yet he must, at all times, show all possible respect for the uniform that he wears and the great nation that he represents. If a midshipman permits himself to be led into scrapes that many college boys regard as merely "larks," he is considered a disgrace to the Naval service.

Always, at home and abroad, the "middy" must maintain his own dignity and that of his country and service. Should he fail seriously, he is regarded by his superiors and by the Navy Department as being unfit to defend the honor of his flag.

The wildest group from the summer practice fleet was that made up of Pennington and his friends. Pen received more money in France from his fond but foolish father. Wherever Pennington's group went, they cut a wide swath of "sport," though they did nothing actually dishonorable. Yet they were guilty of many pranks which, had the midshipmen been caught, would have resulted in demerits.

Ports in France, Spain, Portugal and Italy were touched briefly. At some of these ports the midshipmen received much attention.

But at last the fleet turned back past Gibraltar, and stood on for the Azores, the last landing point before reaching home.

When two nights out from Gibraltar a sharp summer gale overtook the fleet. Even the huge battleships labored heavily in the seas, the "Massachusetts" bringing up the rear.

She was in the same position when the morning broke. The midshipmen, after breakfast, enjoyed a few minutes on the deck before going below for duty in the engine rooms, the dynamo room, the "stoke hole" and other stations.

Suddenly, from the stern rail, there went up the startled cry:

"Man overboard!"

In an instant the marine sentry had tumbled two life–preservers over into the water.

With almost the swiftness of telegraphy the cry had reached the bridge. Without stopping to back the engine the big battleship's helm was thrown hard over, and the great steel fighting craft endeavored to find her own wake in the angry waters with a view to going back over it.

Signal men broke out the news to the flagship. The other two great battleships turned and headed back in the interests of humanity.

It seemed almost as though the entire fleet had been swung out of its course by pressure on an electric button.

Officers who were not on duty poured out. The captain was the first to reach the quarter–deck. He strode into the midst of a group of stricken–looking midshipmen.

"Who's overboard!" demanded the commanding officer.

"Hallam, sir——"

"And Darrin, sir——"

"And Dalzell, sir——"

"How many?" demanded the captain sharply.

"Three, sir."

"How did so many fall overboard?"

"Mr. Hallam was frolicking, sir," reported Midshipman Farley, "and lost his footing."

"But Mr. Darrin and Mr. Dalzell?" inquired the captain sharply.

"As soon as they realized it, sir, Darrin and Dalzell leaped overboard to go to Hallam's rescue, sir."

"It's a wonder," muttered the captain, glancing shrewdly at the bronzed, fine young fellows around him, "that not more of you went overboard as well."

"Many of them would, sir," replied Farley, "but an officer forward shouted: 'No more midshipmen go overboard,' So we stopped, sir."

Modest Mr. Farley did not mention the fact that he was running toward the stern, intent on following his chums into the rough sea at the very instant when the order reached him.

The captain, however, paused for no more information. He was now running forward to take the bridge beside the watch officer.

The midshipmen, too, hurried forward, mingling with the crew, as the big battleship swung around and tried to find her wake.

The flagship had crowded on extra steam, and was fast coming over the seas.

With such a sea running, it was well nigh impossible to make out so small a thing as a head or a life-preserver, unless it could be observed at the instant when it crested a wave.

Marine glasses were in use by every officer who had brought his pair to the deck. Others rushed back to their cabins to get them.

A lieutenant of the marine corps stood forward, close to a big group of sorrowing midshipmen.

"There are certain to be three vacancies in the Naval Academy," remarked the lieutenant.

"Don't say that, sir," begged Farley, in a choking voice. "The three overboard are among the finest fellows in the brigade!"

"I don't want to discourage any of you young gentlemen," continued the marine corps lieutenant. "But there's just about one chance in a thousand that we shall be able to sight and pick up any one of the unlucky three. In the first place, it would take a wonderful swimmer to live long in such a furious sea. In the second place, if all three are still swimming, it will be almost out of the question to make out their heads among the huge waves. You've none of you seen a man overboard before in a big sea?"

Several of the mute, anxious midshipmen shook their heads.

"You'll realize the difficulties of the situation within the next few minutes," remarked the lieutenant. "I am sorry to crush your hopes for your classmates, but this is all a part of the day's work in the Navy."

The largest steam launches from all three of the battleships were being swiftly lowered. Officers and men were lowered with the launches. As the launch shoved off from each battleship tremendous cheers followed them.

"Stop all unnecessary noise!" bellowed the watch officer from the bridge of the "Massachusetts." "You may drown out calls for help with your racket."

While the three battleships went back over their courses in more stately fashion, the launches darted here and there, until it seemed as though they must cover every foot within a square mile.

"I don't see how they can help finding the three," Farley declared hopefully.

"That is," put in another third classman, "if any of the three are still afloat."

"Stow all talk of that sort," ordered Farley angrily.

Other midshipmen joined in with their protests. When a man is overboard in an angry sea all hands left behind try to be optimists.

When fifteen minutes had been spent in the search the onlooking but helpless middies began to look worried.

At the end of half an hour some of them looked haggard. Farley's face was pitiable to see.

At the end of an hour of constant but fruitless searching hardly any one felt any hope of a rescue now.

All three midshipmen, the "man overboard" and his two willing, would–be rescuers, were silently conceded to be drowned.

Yet the hardest blow of all came when, at the end of an hour and a quarter, the flagship signaled the recall of the small boats.

Then, indeed, all hope was given up. In an utter human silence, save for the husky voicing of the necessary orders, the launches were hoisted on board. Then the flagship flew the signal for resuming the voyage.

There were few dry eyes among the third class midshipmen when the battleships fell in formation again and proceeded on their way.

As a result of more signals flown from the flagship, all unnecessary duties of midshipmen for the day were ordered suspended.

In the afternoon the chaplain on each battleship held funeral services over the three lost midshipmen. Officers, middies and crew attended on board each vessel.

CHAPTER IX. THE DESPAIR OF THE "RECALL"

Dave Darrin stood within ten feet of Hallam when that latter midshipman had lost his balance and fallen into the boiling sea.

Dave's spring to the stern rail was all but instantaneous. He was overboard, after his classmate, ere the marine had had time to leap to the life buoys.

Out of the corner of one eye Dan Dalzell saw the marine start on the jump, but Dan was overboard, also, too soon to see exactly what the marine sentry was doing.

Both daring midshipmen sank beneath the surface as they struck.

As Dan came up, however, his hand struck something solid and he clutched at it. It was one of the life buoys.

As he grasped it, and drew his head up a trifle, Dan saw another floating within thirty feet of him. Swimming hard, and pushing, Dan succeeded in reaching the other buoy. He now rested, holding on to both buoys.

"Now, where's David, that little giant?" muttered Dalzell, striving hard to see through the seething waters and over the tops of foam–crested waves.

After a few minutes Dan began to feel decidedly nervous.

"Yet Dave can't have gone down, for he's a better swimmer than I am," was Dan's consoling thought.

At last Dalzell caught sight of another head. He could have cheered, but he expended his breath on something more sensible.

"Dave!" he shouted. "Old Darry! This way! I have the life buoys."

At the same time, holding to both of them, but kicking frantically with his feet, Dalzell managed slowly to push the buoys toward Dave.

Soon after he had started, Dan did utter a cheer, even though it was checked by an inrush of salt water that nearly strangled him.

He saw two heads. Dave Darrin was coming toward him, helping Hallam.

The wind carried the cheer faintly to Dave. He raised his head a little in the water, and caught sight of Dan and the buoys.

Some three minutes it took the two chums to meet. Dave Darrin was all but exhausted, for Hallam was now unconscious.

As Darrin clutched at the buoy he tried to shout, though the voice came weakly:

"Catch hold of Hallam. I'm down and——"

But Dan understood, even before he heard. While Dave clutched at one of the life buoys Dalzell shot out an arm, dragging Hallam in to safety.

Now, it was Darrin who, with both arms, contrived to link the buoys together.

At last the youngsters had a chance to observe the fact that the battleships had put about and were coming back.

"We'll soon be all right," sighed Dave contentedly, as soon as he could speak. "There are thirty-five hundred officers, middies and sailors of the American Navy to look after our safety."

From where they lay as they hung to the buoys the chums could even see the launches lowered.

Dan, with some of the emergency lashing about the buoy, succeeded, after a good deal of effort, and with some aid from Dave, in passing a cord about Hallam and under the latter's armpits that secured that midshipman to one of the buoys. The next move of the chums was to lash the buoys together.

"Now," declared Dave, "we can't lose. We can hang on and be safe here for hours, if need be."

"But what a thundering long time it takes them to bring the battleships around to get to us!" murmured Midshipman Dalzell in wonder.

"Be sure not an unnecessary second has been lost," rejoined Dave. "We're learning something practical now about the handling of big craft."

"I wonder if Hally's a goner?" murmured Dan in an awe–struck voice.

"I don't believe it," Dave answered promptly. "Once we get him back aboard ship the medicos will do a little work over him and he'll sit up and want to know if dinner's ready."

Then they fell silent, for, with the roar of wind and waters, it was necessary for them to shout when they talked.

As the minutes went by slowly, the two conscious midshipmen found themselves filled with amazement.

A dozen times the launches darted by, not far away. It seemed impossible that the keen, restless eyes of the seekers should not discover the imperiled ones.

At such times Dave and Dan shouted with all the power of their lusty young lungs.

Alternately Dan and Dave tried the effect of rising as far as they could and frantically waving an arm. There was not a cap to wave among the three of them.

"I'm beginning to feel discouraged," grunted Dave in disgust at last. "They must have spent a full half day already looking for us."

"Merciful powers!" gasped Dan at last, as they rode half way up the slope of a big wave. "I just caught sight of the 'recall of boats' flying from the flagship!"

"No!" gasped Dave incredulously.

"Yes, I did!"

"But—"

"They've failed and have given up the search," spoke Dan rather despairingly.

"But—"

"We may as well face it," muttered Dan brokenly. "They don't believe that any of us has survived, and we've been abandoned."

"Then," spoke Dave Darrin very coolly, "there's nothing left for us but to die like men of the American Navy."

"It seems heartless, needless," protested Dan.

"No," broke in Darrin. "They've done their best. They're convinced that we're lost. And I should think they would be, after all the time they've searched for us—half a day, at least."

Dan said nothing, but tugged until he succeeded in bringing his watch up to the light.

"The blamed thing is water–logged," he uttered disgustedly.

"Why?"

"The hands point to less than half past nine!"

Darrin managed to get at his own watch.

"My timepiece doesn't call for half past nine, either," he announced.

"Can it be possible—"

"Yes; the time has only seemed longer, I reckon," observed Dalzell.

"Well, we'll face it like men," proposed Dave.

"Of course," nodded Dan. "At least, we're going down in the ocean, and we wear the American Naval uniform. If there's any choice in deaths, I guess that's as good and manly a one as we could choose."

"Poor old Hally won't know much about it, anyway, I guess," remarked Darrin, who seemed unnaturally cool. Possibly he was a bit dazed by the stunning nature of the fate that seemed about to overtake them.

"Maybe the ships will go by us in their final get−away," proposed Dan Dalzell very soberly.

"Not if I'm seaman enough to read the compass by what's visible of the sun," returned Midshipman Darrin.

"Then there's no help for it," answered Dan, choking slightly. "I wonder if we could do anything for Hallam?"

"We won't do anything to bring him to, anyway," muttered Darrin. "Under these circumstances I wouldn't do anything as mean as that to a dog!"

"Maybe he's dead already, anyway," proposed Dan, now hopefully.

"I hope so," came from Darrin.

Now they saw the not very distant battleships alter their courses and steam slowly away.

All was now desolation over the angry sea, as the battleships gradually vanished. The two conscious midshipmen were now resolved to face the end bravely. That was all they could do for themselves and their flag.

CHAPTER X. THE GRIM WATCH FROM THE WAVES

By the time that little more than the mastheads of the departing battleships were visible, Hallam opened his eyes.

It would have seemed a vastly kinder fate had he been allowed to remain unconscious to the last.

Hallam had not been strangled by the inrush of water. In going overboard, this midshipman had struck the water with the back of his head and had been stunned. In the absence of attention he had remained a long time unconscious.

Even now the hapless midshipman whose frollicking had been the cause of the disaster, did not immediately regain his full senses.

"Why, we're all in the water," he remarked after a while.

"Yes," assented Darrin, trying to speak cheerfully.

Midshipman Hallam remained silent for some moments before he next asked:

"How did it happen?"

"Fell overboard," replied Dan laconically, failing to mention who it was who had fallen over the stern.

Again a rather long silence on Hallam's part. Then, at last, he observed:

"Funny how we all fell over at the same time."

To this neither of his classmates made any rejoinder.

"See here," shouted Hallam, after a considerable period of silent wondering, "I remember it all now. I was fooling at the stern rail and I toppled overboard."

Dan nodded without words.

"And you fellows jumped in after me," roared Hallam, both his mental and bodily powers now beginning to return. "Didn't you?"

"Of course," assented Darrin rather reluctantly.

"And what became of the fleet!"

Dave and Dan looked at each other before the former replied:

"Oh, well, Hally, brace up! The ships searched for us a long time, and some launches were put out after us. But they couldn't see our little heads above the big waves, and so——"

"They've gone away and left us?" queried Hallam, guessing at once. "Now, fellows, I don't mind so much for myself, but it's fearful to think that I've dragged you into the same fate. It's awful! Why couldn't you have left me to my fate?"

"Would you have done a thing like that?" demanded Dave dryly.

"Oh, well, I suppose not, but—but—well, I wish I had been left to pay the price of my tomfoolery all alone. It would have served me right. But to drag you two into it—"

Hallam could go no further. He was choking up with honest emotion.

"Don't bother about it, Hally," urged Dave. "It's all in the day's work for a sailor. We'll just take it as it comes, old fellow."

To not one of the trio did it occur to let go of the life buoys and sink as a means of ending misery. In the first place, human instinct holds to hope. In the second place, suicide is the resort of cowards.

"None of you happened to hide any food in his pockets at breakfast, I take it?" asked Dan grimly, at last.

Of course they hadn't.

"Too bad," sighed Dan. "I'm growing terribly hungry."

"Catch a fish," smiled back Darrin.

"And eat it raw?" gasped Dalzell. "Darry, you know my tastes better than that."

"Then wait a few hours longer," proposed Dave, "until even raw fish will be a delicacy."

Hallam took no part in the chaffing. He was miserably conscious, all the while, that his own folly had been solely responsible for the present plight of these noble messmates.

Thus the time passed on. None kept any track of it; they realized only that it was still daylight.

Then suddenly Dave gave a gasp and raised one hand to point.

His two classmates turned and were able to make out the mastheads of a craft in the distance.

How they strained their eyes! All three stared and stared, until they felt tolerably certain that the craft was headed their way.

"They may see us!" cried Hallam eagerly.

"Three battleships and as many launches failed to find us," retorted Dan. "And they were looking for us, too."

As the vessel came nearer and the hull became visible, it took on the appearance of a liner.

"Why, it looks as though she'd run right over us when she gets nearer," cried Dave, his eyes kindling with hope.

"Don't get too excited over it," urged Dan. "For my part, I'm growing almost accustomed to disappointments."

As the minutes passed and the liner came on and on, it looked still more as though she would run down the three middies.

[Illustration: "Look! They See Us!"]

At last, however, the craft was passing, showing her port side, not very far distant, to be sure.

Uniting their voices, the three midshipmen yelled with all their power, even though they knew that their desperate call for help could not carry the distance over the subsiding gale.

Boom! That shot came from the liner, and now her port rail was black with people.

"They see us!" cried Hallam joyously. "Look! That craft is slowing up!"

Once more came the cheers of encouragement, as the liner, now some distance ahead, put off a heavy launch. A masthead lookout, who had first seen the midshipmen, was now signaling the way to the officer in command of the launch.

Unable to see for himself, the officer in the launch depended wholly on those masthead signals. So the launch steamed a somewhat zig–zag course over the waves. Yet, at last, it bore down straight upon the midshipmen.

Darrin, Dalzell and Hallam now came very near to closing their eyes, to lessen the suspense.

A short time more and all three were dragged in over the sides of the launch.

"Get those life buoys in, if you can," begged Dave, as he sank in the bottom of the launch. "They are United States property entrusted to our care."

From officer and seamen alike a laugh went up at this request, but the life buoys were caught with a boathook and drawn aboard.

What rousing cheers greeted the returning launch, from the decks of the liner, "Princess Irene"! When the three midshipmen reached deck and it was learned that they were midshipmen of the United States Navy, the cheering and interest were redoubled.

But the captain and the ship's doctor cut short any attempt at lionizing by rushing the midshipmen to a stateroom containing three berths. Here, under the doctor's orders, the trio were stripped and rubbed down. Then they were rolled into blankets, and hot coffee brought to them in their berths, while their wet clothing was sent below to one of the furnace rooms for hurried drying.

As soon as the medical man had examined them, the steamship's captain began to question them.

"Headed for the Azores, eh?" demanded the ship's master. "We ought to be able to sight your squadron before long."

He hastened out, to give orders to the deck officer.

By the time that the young midshipmen had been satisfactorily warmed, and their clothing had been dried, the ship's surgeon consented to their dressing. After this they were led to a private cabin where a satisfying meal was served them.

"Oh, I don't know," murmured Dan, leaning back, with a contented sigh, after the meal was over; "there are worse things than what happened to us to–day!"

The greater speed of the liner enabled her to sight the battleship squadron something more than two hours afterward. Then the nearest vessel of the fleet was steered for directly.

The deck officers of the liner sent their heavy overcoats for the use of the midshipmen, who, enveloped in these roomy garments, went out on deck to watch the pursuit of their own comrades.

Within another hour it was possible to signal, and from the "Princess Irene's" masthead the signal flags were broken out.

"Now, watch for excitement on board your own craft," smiled the liner's commander, an Englishman.

As soon as the liner's signal had been read by the vessels of the squadron a wild display of signal bunting swiftly broke out.

"Heaven be thanked!" read one set of signal flags.

"We have officially buried the young men, but ask them to go on living," read another.

While the most practical signal of all was:

"The 'Massachusetts' will fall astern of the squadron. Kindly stand by to receive her launch."

In a few minutes more the two vessels were close enough. Both stopped headway. One of the big battleship's launches put off and steamed over, rolling and pitching on the waves.

Most carefully indeed the three midshipmen climbed down a rope ladder and were received by an ensign from the "Massachusetts," who next gave the American Navy's profound thanks to the rescuers of the middies.

"Kindly lower that United States property that was in our care, sir!" Dave Darrin called up.

There was good–humored laughter above, and a look of amazement on Ensign White's face until the two buoys, attached to lines, were thrown down over the side.

"When your time comes you will make a very capable officer, I believe, Mr. Darrin, judging by your care of government property," remarked Ensign White, working hard to keep down the laughter.

"I hope to do so, sir," Dave replied, saluting.

Then away to the "Massachusetts" the launch bore, while the whole battleship squadron cheered itself hoarse over the happy outcome of the day.

Dave, Dan and Hallam all had to do a tremendous amount of handshaking among their classmates when they had reached deck. Pennington was the only one who did not come forward to hold his hand out to Darrin—a fact that was noted at the time by many of the youngsters.

To the captain the trio recounted what had befallen them, as matter for official record.

"Mr. Darrin and Mr. Dalzell," announced the battleship's captain, "I must commend you both for wholly heroic conduct in going to the aid of your classmate. And, Mr. Darrin, I am particularly interested in your incidental determination to preserve government property—the life buoys that you brought back with you."

"It's possible I may need them again, sir," returned Dave, with a smile, though he had no notion of prophetic utterance.

CHAPTER XI. MIDSHIPMAN PENNINGTON'S ACCIDENT

The stop at the Azores was uneventful. It remained in the minds of the midshipmen only as a pleasant recollection of a quaint and pretty place.

Once more the squadron set sail, and now the homeward–bound pennant was flying. The course lay straight across the Atlantic to the entrance of Chesapeake Bay.

On the second night out the wind was blowing a little less than half a gale.

Darkness had fallen when Dave, Dan, Farley and several other midshipmen gathered to talk in low tones at the stern rail.

Presently all of them wandered away but Dave. He stood close to the rail, enjoying the bumping motion every time the descending stern hit one of the rolling waves.

Presently, thinking he saw a light astern, he raised himself, peering astern.

Another group of restless middies had sauntered up. Pennington, after a swift look at the pacing officer in charge here, and discovering that the officer's back was turned, executed a series of swift cartwheels.

"Look out, Pen!" called Midshipman Dwight, in a low, though sharp voice.

Just too late the warning came.

As Pen leaped to his feet after the last turn, one of his hands struck Darrin forcefully.

Dave swayed, tried to clutch at something, then—

"O−o−o−oh!" rang the first startled chorus.

Then, instantly, on top of it, came the rousing hail:

"Man overboard—astern!"

Farley and Hallam were the first to reach the rail. But Lieutenant Burton was there almost as quickly.

"Haul back!" commanded the lieutenant sternly. "No one go overboard!"

That held the middies in check, for in no place, more than in the Navy, are orders orders.

Clack! was the sound that followed the first cry. Like a flash the marine sentry had thrown his rifle to the deck. A single bound carried him to one of the night life buoys. This he released, and hurled far astern.

As the night buoy struck the water a long−burning red light was fused by contact. The glow shone out over the waters.

In the meantime, the "Massachusetts's" speed was being slowed rapidly, and a boat's crew stood at quarters.

The boat put off quickly, guided by the glow of the red signal light on the buoy. Ere the boat reached the buoy the coxswain made out the head and shoulders of a young man above the rim of the floating buoy.

Soon after the boat lay alongside. Dave, with the coxswain's aid, pulled himself into the small craft.

Recovering the buoy, the coxswain flashed the red light three times. From the deck of the battleship came a cheering yell sent up from hundreds of throats.

In the meantime, however, while the boat was on its way to the buoy, a pulsing scene had been enacted on board.

Farley went straight up to Midshipman Pennington.

"Sir," demanded Farley hotly, "why did you push Mr. Darrin over the rail."

Pennington looked at his questioner as one stunned.

"I—I did push Darrin over," admitted Pennington, "but it was an accident."

"An easily contrived one, wasn't it?" demanded Midshipman Farley, rather cynically.

"It was pure accident," contended Pennington, paling. "Until it happened I hadn't the least idea in the world that I was going to send Mr. Darrin or anyone else overboard."

"Huh!" returned Farley dubiously.

"Huh!" quoth Hallam.

Dan Dalzell uttered not a word, but the gaze of his eyes was fixed angrily on Pennington.

That latter midshipman turned as white as a sheet. His hands worked as though he were attempting to clutch at something to hold himself up.

"Surely, you fellows don't believe, do you—" he stammered weakly, then paused.

"One thing we did notice, the other day," continued Farley briskly, "was that, when Darrin was rescued from the sea and returned to us, you were about the only member of the class who didn't go up to him and congratulate him on his marvelous escape."

"How could—"

"Mr. Pennington, I haven't the patience to talk with you now," rejoined Farley, turning on his heel.

At that moment the yell started among the midshipmen nearer the rail. Farley, Dan, Hallam and others joined in the yell and rushed to better points of vantage.

Pennington tried to join in the cheer, but his tongue seemed fixed to the roof of his mouth. He stood clenching and unclenching his hands, his face an ashen gray in his deep humiliation.

"I don't care what one or two fellows may say," groaned Pennington. "But I don't want the class to think such things of me."

He was the most miserable man on board as the small boat came alongside. The boat, occupants and all, was hoisted up to the davits and swung in–board. To the officer of the deck, who stood near–by, Dave turned, with a brisk salute.

"I beg to report that I've come aboard, sir," Darrin uttered.

"And very glad we are of it, Mr. Darrin," replied the officer. "You will go to your locker, change your clothing and then report to the captain, sir."

"Aye, aye, sir."

With another salute, Dave hastened below, followed by Dan Dalzell, who was intent on attending him.

Ten minutes later Dave appeared at the door of the captain's cabin. Just a few minutes after that he came out on deck.

A crowd gathered about him, expressing their congratulations.

"Thank you all," laughed Dave, "but don't make so much over a middy getting a bath outside of the schedule."

To the rear hung Pennington, waiting his chance. At last, as the crowd thinned, Pennington made his way up to Dave.

"Mr. Darrin, I have to apologize for my nonsense, which was the means of pushing you overboard. It was purely accidental, on my honor. I did not even know it was you at the stern, nor did I realize that my antics would result in pushing any one overboard. I trust you will do me the honor of believing my statement."

"Of course I believe it, Mr. Pennington," answered Darrin, opening his eyes.

"There are some," continued Pennington, "who have intimated to me their belief that I did it on purpose. There may be others who half believe or suspect that I might, or would, do such a thing."

"Nonsense!" retorted Dave promptly. "There may be differences, sometimes, between classmates, but there isn't a midshipman in the Navy who would deliberately try to drown a comrade. It's a preposterous insult against midshipman honor. If I hear any one make a charge like that, I'll call him out promptly."

"Some of your friends—I won't name them—insisted, or at least let me feel the force of their suspicions."

"If any of my friends hinted at such a thing, it was done in the heat of the moment," replied Dave heartily. "Why, Mr. Pennington, such an act of dishonor is impossible to a man bred at Annapolis."

Darrin fully believed what he said. On the spur of the moment he held out his hand to his enemy.

Pennington flushed deeply, for a moment, then put out his own hand, giving Dave's a hearty, straightforward grasp.

"I was the first to imply the charge," broke in Farley quickly. "I withdraw it, and apologize to both of you."

There was more handshaking.

During the next few days, while Darry and Pen did not become by any means intimate, they no longer made any effort to avoid each other, but spoke frankly when they met.

The remaining days of the voyage passed uneventfully enough, except for a great amount of hard work that the middies performed as usual.

On the twenty–second of August they entered Chesapeake Bay. Once well inside, they came to anchor. There was considerable practice with the sub–caliber and other smaller guns. On the twenty–ninth of August the battleship fleet returned to the familiar waters around Annapolis. The day after that the young men disembarked.

Then came a hurried skeltering, for the first, second and third classmen were entitled to leave during the month of September.

CHAPTER XII. BACK IN THE HOME TOWN

Back in the old, well–known streets of their home town, Gridley!

Dave and Dan, enjoying every minute of their month's leave, had already greeted their parents, and had told them much of their life as midshipmen.

What hurt was the fact that the skipper of the "Princess Irene" had already told the marine reporters in New York the thrilling story of how Dave and Dan had nearly come to their own deaths rescuing Midshipman Hallam.

Everyone in Gridley, it seemed, had read that newspaper story. Darrin and Dalzell, before they had been home twelve hours, were weary of hearing their praises sung.

"There go two of the smartest, finest boys that old Gridley ever turned out," citizens would say, pointing after Dave and Dan. "They're midshipmen at Annapolis; going to be officers of the Navy one of these days."

"But what's the matter with Dick Prescott and Greg Holmes? They're at West Point."

"Oh, they're all right, too, of course. But Darrin and Dalzell——"

It was the old circumstance of being "the lions of the minute" and of being on the spot.

On the first morning of his arrival home Dave Darrin went frankly and openly to call on his old schoolgirl sweetheart, Belle Meade.

Dan, having no particular associations with the gentler sex, took a stroll around town to meet any old friends who might care to see him again.

Dave was shown into the parlor at the Meade home. Soon after Belle came swiftly in, her face beaming with delight.

"Oh, but you're not in uniform!" was her first disappointed comment.

"No," smiled Dave. "I'm allowed every possible chance, for one month, to forget every detail of the big grind which for a short time I've left behind."

"But you're the same old Dave," cried Belle, "only bigger and manlier. And that magnificent work you and Dan did in jumping over–bo——"

"Stop!" begged Dave. "You're a friend of mine, aren't you! Then don't add to the pain that has been already inflicted on me. If I had had the newspapers in mind I wouldn't have the nerve to——But please let's not talk about it anymore."

Then the two young people seated themselves and spent a delightful hour in talking over all that had befallen them both since they had last met.

Belle, too, through Laura Bentley, had some much later news of the old chums, Dick and Greg, now cadets at West Point.

This news, however, will be found in full in "DICK PRESCOTT'S SECOND YEAR AT WEST POINT."

"What are your plans for this afternoon?" Belle asked at last.

"That's what I want your help in making," Dave answered.

"Can you get hold of Dan?"

"No trouble about that. But keeping hold of him may be more difficult," laughed Dave.

"I was going to propose that you get Dan, call here and then we'll all go over to Laura Bentley's. I know she'll be anxious to see us."

"Nothing could be better in the way of a plan," assented Dave. "I'll pin Danny boy down to that. It would really seem like a slight on good old Dick if we didn't make Laura an early call."

"I'll go to the telephone, now, and tell her that we're coming," cried Belle, rising quickly.

"Laura is delighted," she reported, on her return to the room. "But Dave, didn't you at least bring along a uniform, so that we could see what it looks like?"

"I didn't," replied Dave, soberly, then added, quizzically:

"You've seen the district messenger boys on the street, haven't you?"

"Yes, of course; but what—"

"Our uniforms look very much like theirs," declared Dave.

"I'm afraid I can't undertake to believe you," Belle pouted.

"Well, anyway, you girls will soon have a chance to see our uniforms. Just as soon as our hops start, this fall, you and Laura will come down and gladden our hearts by letting us drag you, won't you!"

"Drag us?" repeated Belle, much mystified.

"Oh, that's middies' slang for escorting a pretty girl to a midshipman hop."

"You have a lot of slang, then, I suppose."

"Considerable," admitted Dave readily.

"What, then, is your slang for a pretty girl?"

"Oh, we call her a queen."

"And a girl who is—who isn't—pretty!"

"A gold brick," answered Dave unblushingly.

"A gold brick?" gasped Belle. "Dear me! 'Dragging a gold brick' to a hop doesn't sound romantic, does it?"

"It isn't," Darrin admitted.

"Yet you have invited me—"

"Our class hasn't started in with its course of social compliments yet," laughed Dave. "Please go look in the glass. Or, if you won't believe the glass, then just wait and see how proud Dan and I are if we can lead you and Laura out on the dancing floor."

"But what horrid slang!" protested Belle. "The idea of calling a homely girl a gold brick! And I thought you young men received more or less training in being gracious to the weaker sex."

"We do," Dave answered, "as soon as we can find any use for the accomplishment. Fourth classmen, you know, are considered too young to associate with girls. It's only now, when we've made a start in the third class, that we're to be allowed to attend the hops at all."

"But why must you have to have such horrid names for girls who have not been greatly favored in the way of looks? It doesn't sound exactly gallant."

"Oh, well, you know," laughed Dave, "we poor, despised, no–account middies must have some sort of sincere language to talk after we get our masks off for the day. I suppose we like the privilege, for a few minutes in each day, of being fresh, like other young folks."

"What is your name for 'fresh' down at Annapolis!" Belle wanted to know.

"Touge."

"And for being a bit worse than touge?"

"Ratey."

"Which did they call you?" demanded Belle.

Dave started, then sat up straight, staring at Miss Meade.

"I see that your tongue hasn't lost its old incisiveness," he laughed.

"Not among my friends," Belle replied lightly. "But I can't get my mind off that uniform of yours that you didn't bring home. What would have happened to you if you had been bold enough to do it?"

"I guess I'd have 'frapped the pap,'" hazarded Dave.

"And what on earth is 'frapping the pap'?" gasped Belle.

"Oh, that's a brief way of telling about it when a midshipman gets stuck on the conduct report."

"I'm going to buy a notebook," asserted Belle, "and write down and classify some of this jargon. I'd hate to visit a strange country, like Annapolis, and find I didn't know the language. And, Dave, what sort of place is Annapolis, anyway?"

"Oh, it's a suburb of the Naval Academy," Dave answered.

"Is it dreadfully hard to keep one's place in his class there?" asked Belle.

"Well, the average fellow is satisfied if he doesn't 'bust cold,'" Dave informed her.

"Gracious! What sort of explosion is 'busting cold'?"

"Why, that means getting down pretty close to absolute zero in all studies. When a fellow has the hard luck to bust cold the superintendent allows him all his time, thereafter, to go home and look up a more suitable job than one in the Navy. And when a fellow bilges——"

"Stop!" begged Belle. "Wait!"

She fled from the room, to return presently bearing the prettiest hat that Dave ever remembered having seen on her shapely young head. In one hand she carried a dainty parasol that she turned over to him.

"What's the cruise?" asked Darrin, rising.

"I'm going out to get that notebook, now. Please don't talk any more 'midshipman' to me until I get a chance to set the jargon down."

As she stood there, such a pretty and wholesome picture, David Darrin thought he never before had seen such a pretty girl, nor one dressed in such exquisite taste. Being a boy, it did not occur to him that Belle Meade had been engaged for weeks in designing this gown and others that she meant to wear during his brief stay at home.

"What are you thinking of?" asked Belle.

"What a pity it is that I am doomed to a short life," sighed Darrin.

"A short life? What do you mean?" Belle asked.

"Why, I'm going to be assassinated, the first hop that you attend at the Naval Academy."

"So I'm a gold brick, am I?" frowned Belle.

"You—a—gold brick?" stammered Dave. "Why, you—oh, go look in the glass!"

"Who will assassinate you?"

"A committee made up from among the fellows whose names I don't write down on your dance card. And there are hundreds of them at Annapolis. You can't dance with them all."

"I don't intend to," replied Belle, with a toss of her head. "I'll accept, as partners, only those who appear to me the handsomest and most distinguished looking of the midshipmen. No one else can write his name on my card."

"Dear girl, I'm afraid you don't understand our way of making up dance cards at Crabtown."

"Where?"

"Crabtown. That's our local name for Annapolis."

"Gracious! Let me get out quickly and get that notebook!"

"At midshipmen's hops the fellow who drags the——"

"Gold brick," supplied Belle, resignedly.

"No—not for worlds! You're no gold brick, Belle, and you know it, even though you do refuse to go to the mirror. But the fellow who drags any femme—"

"Please—?"

"'Femme' stands for girl. The fellow who drags any femme makes up her dance card for her."

"And she hasn't a word to say about it?"

"Not as a rule."

"Oh!" cried Belle, dramatically.

She moved toward the door. Dave, who could not take his eyes from her pretty face, managed, somehow, to delay her.

"Belle, there's something—" he began.

"Good gracious! Where? What?" she cried, looking about her keenly.

"It's something I want to say—must say," Dave went on with more of an effort than anyone but himself could guess.

"Tell me, as we're going down the street," invited Belle.

"*Wha—a—at?*" choked Dave. "Well, I guess not!"

He faced her, resting both hands lightly on her shoulders.

"Belle, we were pretty near sweethearts in the High School, I think," he went on, huskily, but looking her straight in the eyes. "At least, that was my hope, and I hope, most earnestly, that it's going to continue. Belle, I am a long way from my real career, yet. It will be five years, yet, before I have any right to marry. But I want to look forward, all the time, to the sweet belief that my schoolgirl sweetheart is going to become my wife one of these days. I want that as a goal to work for, along with my commission in the Navy. But to this much I agree: if you say 'yes' now, and find later that you have made a mistake, you will tell me so frankly."

"Poor boy!" murmured Belle, looking at him fully. "You've been a plebe until lately, and you haven't been allowed to see any girls. I'm not going to take advantage of you as heartlessly as that."

Yet something in her eyes gave the midshipman hope.

"Belle," he continued eagerly, "don't trifle with me. Tell me—will you marry me some day?"

Then there was a little more talk and—well, it's no one's business.

"But we're not so formally engaged," Belle warned him, "that you can't write me and draw out of the snare if you wish when you're older. And I'm not going to wear any ring until you've graduated from the Naval Academy. Do you understand that, Mr. David Darrin?"

"It shall be as you say, either way," Dave replied happily.

"And now, let us get started, or we shan't get out on the street to–day," urged Belle.

Then they passed out on the street, and no ordinarily observant person would have suspected them of being anything more than school friends.

Being very matter–of–fact in some respects, Belle's first move was to go to a stationer's, where she bought a little notebook bound in red leather.

Dave tried to pay for that purchase, but Belle forestalled him.

"Why didn't you allow me to make you that little gift?" he asked in a low tone, when they had reached the street.

"Wait," replied Belle archly. "Some day you may find your hands full in that line."

"One of my instructors at Annapolis complimented me on having very capable hands," Dave told her dryly.

"The instructor in boxing?" asked Belle.

It was a wonderfully delightful stroll that the middy and his sweetheart enjoyed that September forenoon.

Once Dave sighed, so pronouncedly that Belle shot a quick look of questioning at him.

"Tired of our understanding already?" she demanded.

"No; I was thinking how sorry I am for Danny boy! He doesn't know the happiness of having a real sweetheart."

"How do you know he doesn't?" asked Belle quickly. "Does he tell you everything?"

"No; but I know Danny's sea-going lines pretty well. I'd suspect, at least, if he had a sweetheart."

"Are you sure that you would?"

"Oh, yes! By gracious! There's Danny going around the corner above at this very moment."

Belle had looked in the same instant.

"Yes; and a skirt swished around the corner with him," declared Belle impressively. "It would be funny, wouldn't it, if you didn't happen to know all about Dan Dalzell?"

In the early afternoon, however, the mystery was cleared up.

On the street Dalzell had encountered Laura Bentley. Both were full of talk and questions concerning Dick Prescott and Greg Holmes, at West Point, for which reason Dan had strolled home with Miss Bentley without any other thought, on the midshipman's part, than playing substitute gallant for his chum, Cadet Richard Prescott, U.S. Military Academy.

A most delightful afternoon the four young people spent together at the Bentley home.

These were the forerunners of other afternoons.

Belle and Laura, however, were not able to keep their midshipmen to themselves.

Other girls, former students at the High School, arranged a series of affairs to which the four young people were invited.

Dave Darrin's Second Year at Annapolis

Dave's happiest moments were when he had Belle to himself, for a stroll or chat.

Dan's happiest moments, on the other hand, were when he was engaged in hunting the old High School fellows, or such of them as were now at home. For many of them had entered colleges or technical schools. Tom Reade and Harry Hazelton, of the famous old Dick &Co., of High School days, were now in the far southwest, under circumstances fully narrated in "THE YOUNG ENGINEERS IN ARIZONA," the second volume of "THE YOUNG ENGINEERS' SERIES.'"

Day by day Belle jotted down in her notebook more specimens of midshipman slang.

"I shall soon feel that I can reel off the language like a native of Crabtown," she confided laughingly to Dare.

"It won't be very long before you have an opportunity to try," Dave declared, "if you and Laura embrace your first opportunity to come to a middy hop."

Dan had a happy enough time of it, even though Dave's suspicion was true in that Dan had no sweetheart. That, however, was Dan's fault entirely, as several of the former High School girls would have been willing to assure him.

Since even the happiest times must all end so the latter part of September drew near.

Then came the day when Dave and Dan met at the railway station. A host of others were there to see them off, for the midshipmen still had crowds of friends in the good old home town.

A ringing of bells, signaling brakesmen, a rolling of steel wheels and the two young midshipmen swung aboard the train, to wave their hats from the platform.

Gridley was gone—lost to sight for another year. Dan was exuberant during the first hour of the journey, Dave unusually silent.

"You need a vast amount of cheering up, David, little giant!" exclaimed Dalzell.

"Oh, I guess not," smiled Dave Darrin quietly, adding to himself, under his breath:

"I carry my own good cheer with me, now."

Lightly his hand touched a breast pocket that carried the latest, sweetest likeness of Miss Belle Meade.

One journey by rail is much like another to the traveler who pays little heed to the scenery.

At the journey's end two well—rested midshipmen joined the throng of others at Crabtown.

CHAPTER XIII. DAN RECEIVES A FEARFUL FACER

"Oh, you heap!" sighed Dan Dalzell dismally.

He sat in his chair, in their new quarters in Bancroft Hall, United States Naval Academy, gazing in mock despair at the pile of new books that he had just drawn.

These text—books contained the subjects in which a midshipman is required to qualify in his second academic year.

"Been through the books for a first look?" called Dave from behind his own study table.

"Some of 'em," admitted Dalzell. "I'm afraid to glance into the others."

"I've looked in all of my books," continued Darrin, "and I've just come to a startling conclusion."

"What?"

"I'm inclined to believe that I have received a complete set of text—books for the first and second classes."

"No such luck!" grunted Dan, getting up and going over to his chum. "Let me see if you got all the books I did."

Before Dave could prevent it, Dan started a determined over–tossing of the book pile. As he did so, Dan suddenly uncovered a photograph from which a fair, sweet, laughing face gazed up at him.

"Oh, I beg a million pardons, Dave, old boy!" cried Dalzell.

"You needn't," came Dave's frank answer. "I'm proud of that treasure and of all it means to me."

"And I'm glad for you, David, little giant."

Their hands met in hearty clasp, and that was all that was said on that subject at the time.

"But, seriously," Dan grumbled on, after a while, "I'm aghast at what an exacting government expects and demands that we shall know. Just look over the list—mechanical drawing and mechanical processes, analytical geometry, calculus, physics, chemistry, English literature, French and Spanish, integral calculus, spherical trigonometry, stereographic projection and United States Naval history! David, my boy, by the end of this year we'll know more than college professors do."

"Aren't you getting a big head, Danny?" queried Darrin, looking up with a smile.

"I am," assented Dalzell, "and I admit it. Why, man alive, one has to have a big head here. No small head would contain all that the Academic Board insists on crowding into it."

By the time that the chums had attended the first section recitations on the following day, their despair was increased.

"Davy, I don't see how we are ever going to make it, this year," Dalzell gasped, while they were making ready for supper formation. "We'll bilge this year without a doubt."

"There's only one reason I see for hoping that we can get through the year with fair credit," murmured Darrin.

"And what's that?"

"Others have done it, before us, and many more are going to do it this year," replied Dave slowly, as he laid comb and brush away and drew on his uniform blouse.

"I know men have gotten through the Naval Academy in years gone by," Dalzell agreed. "But, the first chance that I have, I'm going to look the matter up and see whether the middies of old had any such fearful grind as we have our noses held to."

"Oh, we'll do it," declared Darrin confidently. "I shall, anyway—for I've got to!"

As he spoke he was thinking of Belle Meade, and of her prospects in life as well as his own.

As the days went by, however, Dave and Dan became more and more dull of spirits. The grind was a fearful one. A few very bright youngsters went along all right, but to most of the third classmen graduation began to look a thousand years away.

The football squad was out now and training in deadly earnest. There were many big games to be played, but most of all the middies longed to tow West Point's Army eleven into the port of defeat.

In their first year Dave and Dan had looked forward longingly to joining the gridiron squad. They had even practised somewhat. But now they realized that playing football in the second year at Annapolis must be, for them, merely a foolish dream.

"I'm thankful enough if I can study day and night and keep myself up to 2.5," confessed Darrin, as he and Dan chatted over their gridiron longings.

Two–and–five tenths is the lowest marking, on a scale of four, that will suffice to keep a midshipman in the Naval Academy.

"I'm not going to reach 2.5 in some studies this month," groaned Dan. "I know that much by way of advance information. The fates be thanked that we're allowed until the semi–ans to pick up. But the question is, are we ever going to pick up? As I look through my books it seems to me that every succeeding lesson is twice as hard as the one before it."

"Other men have gone through, every year."

"And still other men have been dropped every year," Dalzell dolefully reminded him.

"We're among those who are going to stay," Dave contended stubbornly.

"Then I'm afraid we'll be among those who are dropped after Christmas and come back, next year, as bilgers," Dalzell groaned.

"Now, drop that!" commanded Darrin, almost roughly. "Remember one thing, Daniel little lion slayer! My congressman and your senator won't appoint us again, if we fail now. No talk of that kind, remember. We've got to make our standing secure within the next few weeks."

Before the month was over the football games began in earnest on the athletic field. Darrin and Dalzell, however, missed every game. They were too busy poring over their text–books. Fortunately for them their drills, parades and gym. work furnished them enough exercise.

The end of October found Darrin at or above 2.5 in only three studies. Dan was above 2.5 in two studies—below that mark in all others.

"It's a pity my father never taught me to swear," grumbled Dalzell, in the privacy of their room.

"Stow that talk," ordered Darrin, "and shove off into the deeper waters of greater effort."

"Greater effort?" demanded Dan, in a rage. "Why I study, now, every possible moment of the time allowed for such foolishness. And we can't run a light. Right after taps the electric light is turned off at the master switch."

"We're wasting ninety seconds of precious time, now, in grumbling," uttered Dave, seating himself doggedly at his study table.

"Got any money, Darry?" asked Dalzell suddenly.

"Yes; are you broke?"

"I am, and the next time I go into Annapolis I mean to buy some candles."

"Don't try that, Danny. Running a light is dangerous, and doubly so with candles. The grease is bound to drip, and to be found in some little corner by one of the discipline officers. It would be no use to study if you are going to get frapped on the pap continuously."

Immediately after supper both midshipmen forfeited their few minutes of recreation, going at once back to their study tables. There they remained, boning hard until the brief release sounded before taps was due.

Almost at the sound of the release there came a knock at the door. Farley and his roommate, Page, came bounding in.

"I've got to say something, or I'll go daffy," cried Farley, rubbing his eyes. "Fellows, did you ever hear of such downright abuse as the second year course of studies means?"

"It is tough," agreed Dave. "But what can we do about it, except fight it out?"

"Can you make head or tail out of calculus?" demanded Farley.

"No," admitted Darrin, "but I hope to, one of these days."

Just then Freeman, of the first class, poked his head in, after a soft knock.

"What is this—a despair meeting?" he called cheerily.

"Yes," groaned Page. "We're in a blue funk over the way recitations are going."

"Oh, buck up, kiddies!" called Freeman cheerily, as he crossed the floor. "Youngsters always get in the doldrums at the beginning of the year."

"You're a first classman. When you were in the third class did you have all the studies that we have now?"

"Every one of them, sir," affirmed Midshipman Freeman gravely, though there was a twinkle in his eyes.

"And did you come through the course easily?" asked Page.

"Not easily," admitted the first classman. "There isn't anything at Annapolis that is easy, except the dancing. In fact, during the first two months very few of our class came along like anything at all. After that, we began to do better. By the time that semi−ans came around nearly all of us managed to pull through. But what seems to be the worst grind of all—the real blue paint?"

"Calculus!" cried the four youngsters in unison.

"Why, once you begin to see daylight in calculus it's just as easy as taking a nap," declared the first classman.

"At present it seems more like suffering from delirium," sighed Dave.

"What's the hard one for to−morrow?" asked Freeman.

"Here it is, right here," continued Dave, opening his text−book. "Here's the very proposition."

The others crowded about, nodding.

"I remember that one," laughed Freeman lightly. "Our class named it 'sticky fly paper.'"

"It was rightly named," grumbled Farley.

"None of you four youngsters see through it?" demanded Midshipman Freeman.

"Do you mean to claim, sir, that you ever did?" insisted Dan Dalzell.

"Not only once, but now," grinned Mr. Freeman. "You haven't been looking at this torturing proposition from the right angle—that's all. Now, listen, while I read it."

"Oh, we all know how it runs, Mr. Freeman," protested Page.

"Nevertheless, listen, while I read it."

As the first classman read through the proposition that was torturing them he threw an emphasis upon certain words that opened their eyes better as to the meaning.

"Now, it works out this way," continued the first classman, bending over the disk and drawing paper and pencil toward him. "In the first place."

Freeman seemed to these youngsters like a born demonstrator. Within five minutes he had made the "sticky fly paper" problem so plain to them all that they glanced from one to another in astonishment.

"Why, it does seem easy," confessed Farley.

"It sounds foolish, now," grinned Darrin. "I'm beginning to feel ashamed of myself."

"Mr. Freeman," protested Page, "you've saved us from suicide, or some other gruesome fate."

"Then I'll drop in once in a while again," promised the first classman.

"But that will take time from your own studies," remonstrated Darrin generously.

"Not in the least. I won't come around before release. By the time a fellow reaches the first class, if he's going to graduate anyway, he doesn't have to study as hard as a youngster does. The man who reaches the first class has had all the habits of true study ground into him."

Darrin, Dalzell, Farley and Page were all in different sections in mathematics. When they recited, next day, it so happened that each was the man to have the "sticky fly paper" problem assigned to him by the instructor. Each of the quartette received a full "4" for the day's marking.

"Did you have any assistance with this problem, Mr. Darrin?" asked Dave's instructor.

"Yes, sir; a member of the first class tried to make it plain to me last night."

"He appears to have succeeded," remarked the instructor dryly.

There was, however, no discredit attached to having received proper assistance before coming into section.

True to his promise Freeman dropped in every fourth or fifth evening, to see if he could be of any help to the four youngsters. Always he found that he could be.

Even when Thanksgiving came, Dave Darrin did not go to Philadelphia, but remained at the Academy, devoting his time to study.

Dan, in sheer desperation, took in the trip to Philadelphia. He hoped to meet Dick Prescott and Greg Holmes, but they did not come down from West Point.

On the first day of December, Dan Dalzell's name was formally reported by the Academic Board in a report to the superintendent which recommended that Midshipman Dalzell be dropped from the rolls for "inaptitude in his studies."

Poor Dan. It was a staggering blow. Yet it struck Dave Darrin just about as hard.

CHAPTER XIV. THE FIRST HOP WITH THE HOME GIRLS

That report was allowed to reach Dan's ears on a Friday.

On the evening of the day following there was to be a midshipman hop on the floor of the great gym.

Moreover, it was the very hop that Belle Meade and Laura Bentley had finally selected to attend. Mrs. Meade was coming with the girls as chaperon.

"Oh, but I shall feel fine and light hearted for going to the dance!" muttered Dan miserably. "Facing the kick–off from the Academy, and doing the light hearted and the fantastic toe with the girls."

"I shan't feel a whole lot more merry myself," sighed Dave, as he gazed affectionately, wistfully at his chum. "Danny, this has hit me about as hard as it has you. And it warns me, too, that my turn will probably come next. I don't stand an awful lot higher in my markings than you do."

"Doesn't it feel fine to be a bilger?" gulped Dalzell, staring at the floor.

A "bilger," as has been already explained, is a midshipman who has failed and has been dropped.

"Oh, but you're not a bilger, yet!" cried Darrin, leaping up and resting both hands on his chum's shoulder.

"What's the odds?" demanded Dan grimly. "I shall be, after I've been before the Board next Monday forenoon at ten o'clock."

"Nonsense! Not if you make a good fight!"

"Fight—nothing!" sighed Dan wearily. "In a fight there's some one else that you can hit back at. But I won't have a blessed soul to fight. I'm up against a gang who are all referees, and all down on me at the outset."

"Nonsense," combatted Dave. "You——"

"Oh, that's all right, David, little giant," returned Dalzell with an attempt at cheeriness. "You mean well, but a fellow isn't reported deficient unless he's so far behind that the Board has his case settled in advance. From all I can hear it isn't once in a camel's age that a fellow so reported, and ordered before the Board, gets off with anything less than a hard, wet bilge. What I'm thinking of now is, what am I going to pick up as a career when I go home from here as a failure."

If it hadn't been for the pride he felt in still having the uniform on, Dalzell might not have been able to check the tears that tried to flow.

"Come on," commanded Dave, leaping up, "we'll run up to the deck above, and see if we can't find Mr. Freeman in."

100

"What good will that do?" demanded Dan. "Freeman is a first classman, but he hasn't any particular drag with the Board."

"It won't do any harm, anyway, for us to have a talk with an older classman," argued Dave. "Button your blouse, straighten your hair and come along."

"So it's as bad as that, is it!" asked Freeman sympathetically, after his cheery "come in" had admitted the unhappy youngsters.

"Yes," replied Dave incisively. "Now, the question is, what can be done about it?"

"I wish you had asked me an easier one," sighed the first classman. "You're mighty well liked, all through the Academy, Dalzell, and every one of us will hate to see you go."

"But what can be done to ward off that fate?" insisted Darrin as impatiently as a third classman might speak to a venerable first classman.

"Well, now, I want to think over that," confessed Freeman frankly. "Of course, Dalzell's record, this term, is in black and white, and can't be gainsaid. It's just possible our young friend can put up some line of talk that will extend his time here, and perhaps enable him to pull through. It's a mighty important question, so I'll tell you what we'll do. Of course, the hop comes on for to-morrow night. Let me have until Sunday evening. Meanwhile I'll talk with some of the other fellows of my class. You both come in here Sunday evening, and I'll have the answer for you—if there's any possible way of finding one."

With that the chums had to be content. Expressing their gratitude to this friendly first classman, they withdrew.

That Saturday forenoon Dan did considerably better with the two recitations that he had in hand.

"I got easier questions than usual, I guess," he said to Dave, with a mournful smile.

After Saturday dinner, Dave and Dan, having secured permission to visit in Annapolis, steered their course through the gate, straight up Maryland Avenue, through State Circle and around into Main Street, to the Maryland House.

At the desk they sent up their cards to Mrs. Meade, then stepped into the parlor.

Barely two minutes had passed when Belle and Laura flew downstairs.

"Mother says she'll be down as soon as she fancies you'll care about seeing her," laughed Belle.

"And how are you getting on in your classes?" asked Laura Bentley, glancing straight at unhappy Dan.

Both midshipmen had agreed not to mention a word of Dan's heartache to either of the girls.

Dan gulped hard, though he managed to conceal the fact.

Darrin, however, was ready with the answer:

"Oh, we're having pretty rough sailing, but we're both still in our class."

Which statement was wholly truthful.

"Up at West Point," Laura continued, "Dick told us that the first two years were the hardest for a man to keep his place. I fancy it's just about the same here, isn't it?"

"Just about," Dave nodded. "The first two years are hardest because it takes all that time for a fellow to get himself keyed up to the gait of study that is required in the government academies. But won't you let us talk about something that's really pleasant, girls?" Dave asked, with his charming smile. "Suppose we talk about yourselves. My, but you girls are good to look at!"

After that, the conversation was shifted to lighter subjects.

Even Dan, in the joy of meeting two girl friends from home, began to be less conscious of his load of misery.

Presently Mrs. Meade came down. She chatted with the two fine-looking young midshipmen for a few moments. Then Dave proposed:

"Wouldn't you like us to escort you through the Academy grounds, so that you can get a good idea of the place in daylight?"

"We've been waiting only for you to invite us," rejoined Belle.

For the next two hours the time was passed pleasantly.

But Belle, behind all her light chatter, was unusually keen and observing.

"Is anything wrong with either of you?" she asked Dave suddenly, when this pair were out of easy hearing of the others.

"Why do you ask that?" inquired Dave, looking at her in his direct fashion.

"Why, I may be unnecessarily sensitive, but I can't help feeling that some sort of disaster is hanging over either you or Dan."

"I hope not," replied Darrin evasively.

"Dave, that isn't a direct answer," warned Belle, raising her eyebrows. "Do you consider me entitled to one?"

"Yes. What's the question?"

"Are you in any trouble here?"

"No, I'm thankful to say."

"Then is Dan!"

"Belle, I'd rather not answer that."

"Why——"

"Well, because, if he is, I'd rather not discuss it."

"Has Dan been caught in any scrape?"

"No. His conduct record is fine."

"Then it must be failure in his studies."

Dave did not answer.

"Why don't you tell me?" insisted Belle.

"If anything were in the wind, Belle, we'd rather not tell you and spoil your visit. And don't ask Dan anything about it."

"I think I know enough," went on Belle thoughtfully and sympathetically. "Poor Dan! He's one of the finest of fellows."

"There are no better made," retorted Dave promptly.

"If anything happens to Dan here, dear, I know you will feel just as unhappy about it as if it happened to yourself."

"Mighty close to it," nodded Darrin. "But it would be a double heartbreak for me, if I had to leave."

"Why?"

"On account of the future I've planned for you, Belle."

"Oh, you silly boy, then!" Belle answered, smiling into his eyes. "I believe I have half committed myself to the idea of marrying you when you've made your place in life. But it was Dave Darrin to whom I gave that half promise—not a uniform of any sort. Dave, if anything ever happens that you have to quit here, don't imagine that it's going to make a particle of difference in our understanding."

"You're the real kind of sweetheart, Belle!" murmured Dave, gazing admiringly at her flushed face.

"Did you ever suspect that I wasn't?" asked Miss Meade demurely.

"Never!" declared Midshipman Darrin devoutly. "Nevertheless, it's fine to be reassured once in a while."

"What a great fellow Dan is!" exclaimed Belle a few minutes later. "See how gayly he is chatting with Laura. I don't believe Laura guesses for a moment that Dan Dalzell is just as game a fellow as the Spartan boy of olden times."

CHAPTER XV. A DISAGREEABLE FIRST CLASSMAN

The hop that night was one of the happiest occasions Dave had ever known, yet it was destined to result in trouble for him.

Midshipman Treadwell, of the first class, caught sight of Belle as she entered the gym at Dave Darrin's side.

With Treadwell it happened to be one of those violent though unusually silly affairs known as "love at first sight."

As for Belle, she was not likely to have eyes for anyone in particular, save Dave.

Treadwell, who had come alone, and who was not to be overburdened with dances, went after Dave as soon as that youngster left Belle for the first time.

"Mighty sweet looking girl you have with you, Darry," observed the first classman, though he took pains not to betray too much enthusiasm.

"Right!" nodded Dave.

"You'll present me, won't you?"

"Assuredly, as soon as I come back. I have a little commission to attend to."

"And you might be extremely kind, Darry, and write me down for a couple of numbers on Miss——"

"Miss Meade is the young lady's name."

"Then delight me by writing down a couple of reservations for me on Miss Meade's card."

Darrin's face clouded slightly.

"I'd like to, Treadwell, but the card is pretty crowded, and some other fellows—"

"One dance, anyway, then."

"I will, then, if there's a space to be left, and if Miss Meade is agreeable," promised Dave, as he hurried away.

Two minutes later, when he returned, looking very handsome, indeed, in his short-waisted, gold-laced dress coat, Dave felt his arm touched.

"I'm waiting for you to keep your engagement with me," Midshipman Treadwell murmured.

"Come along; I shall be delighted to present you to Miss Meade."

Since every midshipman is granted to be a gentleman, midshipman etiquette does not require that the lady be consulted about the introduction.

"Miss Meade," began Dave, bowing before his sweetheart, "I wish to present Mr. Treadwell"

Belle's greeting was easy. Treadwell, gazing intensely into her eyes, exchanged a few commonplaces. Belle, entirely at her ease, did not appear to be affected by the battery of Mr. Treadwell's gaze. Then good breeding required that the first classman make another bow and stroll away.

As he left, Treadwell murmured in Dare's ear:

"Don't forget that dance, Darry! Two if there is any show."

Midshipman Darrin nodded slightly. As he turned to Belle, that young lady demanded lightly:

"Is that pirate one of your friends, Dave?"

"Not more so than any other comrades in the brigade," Darrin answered. "Why?"

"Nothing, only I saw you two speaking together a little while ago——"

"That was when he was asking me to present him."

"Then, after you left him," continued Belle, in a low voice, "Mr. Treadwell scowled after you as though he could have demolished you."

"Why, I've no doubt Mr. Treadwell is very jealous of me," laughed Damn happily. "Why shouldn't he be? By the way, will you let me see your dance card? Mr. Treadwell asked me to write his name down for one or two dances."

"Please don't," begged Belle suddenly, gripping her dance card tightly. "I hope you don't mind, Dave," she added in a whisper, "but I've taken just a shadow of a dislike to Mr. Treadwell, after the way that he scowled after you. I—I really don't want to dance with him."

Dave could only bow, which he did. Then other midshipmen were presented. Belle's card was quickly filled, without the appearance of Midshipman Treadwell's name on it.

The orchestra struck up. Dave danced the first two numbers with Belle, moving through a dream of happiness as he felt her waist against his arm, one of her hands resting on his shoulder.

The second dance was a repetition of Dave's pleasure. Then Dave and Dan exchanged partners for two more dances.

After their first dance, a waltz, Dave led Laura to a seat.

"Will you get me a glass of water, Dave?" Laura asked, fanning herself.

As Dave hastened away he felt, once more, a light, detaining touch.

"Darry, did you save those two dances for me with Miss Meade?" asked Treadwell.

"Oh, I'm sorry," Dave replied. "But there had been many other applicants. By the time that Miss Meade's card was filled there were many disappointed ones."

"And I'm one of them?" demanded Mr. Treadwell.

"Very sorry," replied Darrin regretfully, "but you were one of the left–over ones."

"Very good, sir," replied Treadwell coldly, and moved away.

"Now, I'll wager anything that Treadwell is sore with me," murmured Dave to himself. "However, Belle is the one to be pleased."

It was a particularly gay and pleasant hop. When it was over Dave and Dan escorted the girls and Mrs. Meade back to the hotel. The little room in Bancroft Hall seemed especially small and dingy to the returning midshipmen.

Especially was Dan Dalzell in the blues. Though he had been outwardly gay with the girls, he now suffered a re–action. Dave, too, shivered for his friend.

Mrs. Meade and the girls returned by an early morning train, so the two chums did not see the girls again during that visit.

On Sunday, Dave went at his books with a dogged air, after morning chapel and dinner.

"I suppose this is the last day of study for me here," grimaced Dan, "so I mean to make the most of the pleasure."

"Nonsense," retorted Darrin heartily; "you'll finish out this year, and then have two more solid years of study here ahead of you."

"Cut it!" begged Dan dolefully. "Don't try to jolly me along like that."

"You're down in the dumps, just now, Danny boy," smiled Darrin wistfully. "Just bombard the Board with rapid–fire talk to–morrow, and you'll pull through all right."

Dan sighed, then went on with his half–hearted study.

Later in the afternoon Dave, feeling the need of fresh air, closed his books.

"Come for a walk, Danny boy?"

"Don't dare to," replied Dalzell morosely.

So, though Darrin went out, he resolved not to remain long away from his moody chum.

Outside, on one of the cement walks, Dave turned toward Flirtation Walk. It seemed the best surrounding in which to think of Belle.

"Mr. Darrin!" called a voice.

Dave turned, to behold Mr. Treadwell coming at a fast stride with a scowl on his face.

"That was a dirty trick you played me last night, Mr. Darrin!" cried the first classman angrily.

"What?" gasped Dave, astonished, for this was not in line with the usual conversation of midshipmen.

"You know well enough what I mean," cried Treadwell angrily. "You spiked my only chance to dance with Miss Meade."

"You're wrong there," retorted Dave coldly and truthfully "I didn't."

"Then how did it happen?"

"I can't discuss that with you," Darrin rejoined. "I didn't make any effort, though, to spoil your chance of a dance with the young lady."

"Mr. Darrin, I don't choose to believe you, sir!"

Dave's face went crimson, then pale.

"Do you realize what you're saying, Mr. Treadwell?"

"Of course"—sneeringly.

"Are you trying to pick trouble with me!" demanded Dave, his eyes flashing with spirit.

"I repeat that I don't choose to believe your explanation, sir."

"Then you pass me the lie?"

"As you prefer to consider it," jeered the first classman.

"Oh, very good, then, Mr. Treadwell," retorted Dave, eyeing the first classman and sizing him up.

Treadwell was one of the biggest men, physically, in the brigade. He was also one of the noted fighters of his class. Beside Treadwell, Midshipman Darrin did not size up at all advantageously.

"If you do not retract what you just said," pursued Dave Darrin, growing cooler now that he realized the deliberate nature of the affront that had been put upon him, "I shall have no choice but to send my friends to you."

"Delighted to see them, at any time," replied the first classman, turning disdainfully upon his heel and strolling away.

"Now, why on earth does that fellow deliberately pick a fight with me?" wondered Darrin, as he strolled along by himself. "Treadwell can thump me. He can knock me clean down the Bay and into the Atlantic Ocean, but what credit is there in it for a first classman to thrash a youngster?"

It was too big a puzzle. After thinking it over for some time Dave turned and strolled back to Bancroft Hall.

"You didn't stay out long!" remarked Dan, looking up with a weary smile as his chum re-entered their room.

"No," admitted Dave. "There wasn't much fun in being out alone."

With a sigh, Dan turned back to his book, while Dave seated himself at his own study table, in a brown daze.

Things were happening fast—Dan's impending "bilge" from the Naval Academy, and his own coming fight with the first classman who would be sure to make it a "blood fight"!

CHAPTER XVI. HOW DAN FACED THE BOARD

"We trust, Mr. Dalzell, that you can make some statement or explanation that will show that we shall be justified in retaining you as a midshipman in the Naval Academy."

It was the superintendent of the United States Naval Academy who was speaking.

Dan's hour of great ordeal had come upon him. That young midshipman found himself in the Board Room, facing the entire Academic Board, trying to remember what Freeman had told him the night before.

The time was 10.30 a.m. on that fateful Monday.

Midshipman Dalzell appeared to be collected, but he was also very certainly white-faced.

Many a young man, doomed to be sent forth from a Naval career, back into the busy, unheeding world, had faced this Board in times past. So it was hardly to be expected that Dan would inspire any unusual interest in the members of the Board.

Dan swallowed at something hard in his throat, then opened his lips to speak.

"I am aware, sir, and gentlemen, that I am at present sufficiently deficient in my studies to warrant my being dropped," Dan began rather slowly. "Yet I would call attention to the fact that I was nearly as badly off, in the matter of markings, at this time last year. It is also a matter of record that I pulled myself together, later on, and contrived to get through the first year with a considerable margin of credits to spare. If I am permitted to finish the present term here I believe I can almost positively promise that I will round out this year with as good a showing as I did last year."

"You have thought the matter carefully out in making this statement, have you, Mr. Dalzell?" asked the superintendent.

"I have, sir."

"Have you any explanation to offer for falling below the standards so far this year, Mr. Dalzell?"

"I believe, sir, that I make a much slower start, with new studies, than most of my classmates," Dan continued, speaking more rapidly now, but in a most respectful manner. "Once I begin to catch the full drift of new studies I believe that I will overtake some of my classmates who showed a keener comprehension at the first. I think, sir, and gentlemen, that my record, as contrasted with the records of some of my classmates who achieved about the same standing I did for last year will bear my statement out."

[Illustration: "Have You Any Explanation to Offer, Mr. Dalzell?"]

The superintendent turned to a printed pamphlet in which were set forth the records of the midshipmen for the year before.

"Mr. Dalzell," asked another member of the Board, "do you feel that you are really suited for the life of the Navy? Is it your highest ambition to become an officer of the Navy?"

"It's my only ambition, sir, in the way of a career," Dan answered solemnly. "As to my being suited for the Navy, sir, I can't make a good answer to that. But I most earnestly hope that I shall have an opportunity, for the present, to try to keep myself in the service."

"And you feel convinced that you need only to be carried for the balance of the term to enable you to make good, and to justify any action that we may take looking to that end?" asked another member of the Board.

"That is my firm conviction, sir."

The superintendent, who had been silently examining and marking some statements in the pamphlet, now passed it to the nearest member of the Board, who, after a glance or two, passed the pamphlet on to another member.

Silence fell upon the room while Dan's printed record was being read.

"Have you anything else that you wish to say, Mr. Dalzell?" asked the superintendent at last.

"Only this, sir and gentlemen," replied Dan promptly. "If I am permitted to go on with the brigade, I promise, as far as any human being may promise, that I will not only be found to have passed at the end of this term, but that I will also have a higher marking after the annual examinations than after the semi–annuals."

These last few words Dan spoke with his whole soul thrown into the words. How he longed to remain in the Navy, now that he stood at the threshold of the life, uncertain whether he was about to be kicked across it into the outer world!

After glancing around the table, the superintendent turned once more to the young man.

"That will be all, at present, Mr. Dalzell."

Saluting briskly, crisply, Dan wheeled about, marching from the room.

He was in time to make a section recitation before dinner.

"How did you come out, Danny boy?" anxiously inquired Dave Darrin as the two, in their room, hastily prepared to answer the coming call for dinner formation.

"I wish I knew," replied Dalzell wistfully. "I said all that I could say without being everlastingly fresh."

After the brigade had been formed for dinner, and the brigade adjutant had reported the fact, the command was given:

"Publish the orders!"

This the brigade adjutant did rapidly, and in perfunctory tones.

Dalzell jumped, however, when he heard his own name pronounced. He strained his ears as the brigade adjutant read:

"In the matter of Daniel Dalzell, summoned before the Academic Board to determine his fitness and aptitude for continuing in the brigade, the Board has granted Midshipman Dalzell's urgent request that he be continued as a midshipman for the present."

There was a great lump, instantly, in Dan's throat. It was a reprieve, a chance for official life—but that was all.

"I'll make good—I'll make good!" he told himself, with a violent gulp.

The orders were ringing out sharply now. The midshipmen were being marched in to dinner.

Hardly a word did Dalzell speak as he ate. As for Dave Darrin, he was too happy over his chum's respite to want to talk.

Yet, when they strolled together in the open air during the brief recreation period following the meal, Dalzell suddenly asked:

"Dave when do you fight with Treadwell?"

"To-night, I hope," replied Darrin.

"Oh, then I must get busy!"

"Why?"

"Why, I'm to represent you, Darry. Who are Treadwell's—"

"Danny boy, don't make a fuss about it," replied Dave quietly, "but just for this once you are not to be my second."

"Why—"

"Danny boy, you have just gotten by the Board by a hair's breadth. What kind of an act of gratitude would it be for you to make your first act a breach of discipline? For a fight, though often necessary here, is in defiance of the regulations."

"But Dave, I've never been out of your fights!"

"You will be this time, Danny. Don't worry about it, either. Farley and Page are going to stand by me. In fact, I think that even now they are talking with Treadwell's friends."

"You're wrong," murmured Dalzell, looking very solemn. "Here come Farley and Page right now."

In another moment the seconds had reached Darrin and his chum.

"To-night?" asked Dave Quietly.

"Yes," nodded Page.

"Time?"

"Just after recall."

"Good," murmured Darrin. "You two come for me, and I'll be ready. And I thank both of you fellows for taking up the matter for me."

"We'll be mighty glad to be there, Darry," grinned Farley, "for we look to see you finish off that first classman."

"Maybe," smiled Dave quietly. "I'll do all I can, anyway."

"And to think," almost moaned Dan Dalzell, "that you're to be in a scrap, David, little giant, and I'm not to be there to see!"

"There'll be other fights, I'm afraid," sighed Darry. "I seem destined to displease quite a few of the fellows here at Annapolis."

Dan tried to study, that night, after Darrin had left the room in the company of his seconds. Certainly Dan, in the light of his promise made to the Board that morning, had need to study. Yet he found it woefully hard to settle his mind on mathematics while Dave was fighting the fight of his Naval Academy career.

"Oh, well," muttered Dan, picking up a pencil for the third time, "Dave and I each have our own styles of fights, just now. Here goes for a knockout blow at math!"

CHAPTER XVII. LOSING THE TIME–KEEPER'S COUNT

Conners and Brayton were Treadwell's seconds.

Since it is not considered fair to have the referee or time–keeper from either class represented in a fight, Edgerton and Wheeler, of the second class, were referee and time–keeper respectively.

All of the young men were early at the usual fighting ground. The fall air was cool and crisp, but it was not yet considered cold enough to justify the extra risk of holding a fight in–doors.

Dave was quickly stripped and made ready by his seconds. His well–developed chest bespoke fine powers in the way of "wind" and endurance. His smooth, hard, trim muscles stood out distinctly.

Treadwell took more time in getting himself ready for the ring. When at last, however, the first classman stood bared to the waist, he looked like a giant beside Dave Darrin.

"It looks like a shame to take the money, Tread," murmured referee Edgerton.

"I don't want to pound the youngster hard," explained Midshipman Treadwell, in an undertone. "Yet I've got to teach him both to respect my class and myself."

On this point, as an official of the fight, Referee Edgerton did not feel called upon to express an opinion.

Farley, at his first glimpse of the waiting first classman, felt a chill of coming disaster.

"Page," he growled, "that huge top–classman makes our Darry look like a creeping infant."

"Darry will take care of himself," retorted Midshipman Page in an undertone.

"Do you believe it?"

"I surely do."

"But Treadwell looks a whole lot more vast now that he's stripped."

"Darry is much smaller, I know; But Darrin is one of those rare fellows who don't know what it means to be whipped. He can't be put out of business by anything smaller than a twelve–inch gun!"

"I hope you're right," sighed Farley.

Dave, in the meantime, to keep himself from being chilled by the frosty air, was running lightly about, swinging his arms.

"Are you both ready, gentlemen?" inquired Midshipman Edgerton, while Time–keeper Wheeler drew out his stop watch.

Both stepped to toe the scratch.

"Yes." nodded Dave.

"Ready!" rumbled Treadwell.

The referee briefly made the usual announcement about it being a fight to the finish, with two–minute rounds and two minutes between rounds.

"Time!"

As Treadwell leaped forward, both fists in battery, Dave took a swift, nimble sidestep. He felt that he had to study this big fellow carefully before doing more than keep on the defensive.

Now footwork was one of the fighting tricks for which Darry was famous. Yet he had too much courage to rely wholly upon it.

Five times Treadwell swung at his smaller opponent, but each time Dave was somewhere else.

Despite his greater size, Treadwell was himself nimble and an adept at footwork.

Finding it hard, however, to get about as quickly as his smaller opponent, the first classman soon went in for close, in–body fighting, following Dave, half–cornering him, and forcing him to stand and take it.

Two or three body blows Dave succeeded in parrying so that they glanced, doing him little harm.

Then there came an almost crunching sound. Treadwell's right fist had landed, almost dazing the youngster with its weight against his nose.

There was a swift, free rush of the red. Darrin had yielded up "first blood" in the fight.

"I've got to dodge more, and not let myself be cornered," Darrin told himself, keeping his fists busy in warding off blows.

Then, of a sudden, Dave turned on the aggressive. He struck fast and furiously, but Treadwell, with a grin, beat down his attack, then soon landed a swinging hook on Dave's neck that sent him spinning briefly.

"He expects to finish this fight for his own amusement," flashed angrily through Darrin's mind. "I'll get in something that hurts before I toss the sponge."

"Time!"

Two minutes were up. To Dave it seemed more like half an hour.

"Steady, now!" murmured Page, in his principal's ear, as the two seconds leaped at the task of rubbing down their men. "Unless you let yourself get rattled, Darry, that big fellow isn't going to get you. Whenever you're on the defensive, and being crowded hard, change like lightning and drive in for the top classer's solar plexus."

"I tried that three times in this last round," murmured Dave. "But the fellow is too big and powerful for me. He simply pounds me down when I go for him."

"Work for more strategy," whispered Page, as he held a sponge to Dave's battered nose, while Farley rubbed the muscles of his right arm.

"I haven't given up the fight," muttered Dave, "But, of course, I've known from the start that Treadwell is a pretty big fighter for one of my weight."

"Oh, you'll get him yet," spoke Page confidently.

The fighters were being called for the second round.

In this Dave received considerable punishment, though he landed three or four times on Treadwell's body.

Then twice in succession the champion of the third class was knocked down.

Neither, however, was a knockout blow.

Dave took plenty of time, within his rights, about leaping to his feet, and in each instance got away from Treadwell's leaping assault.

Just after the second knock–down, time was called for the end of the round.

"You'll get him yet, Darry," was Page's prediction, but he did not speak as hopefully as before.

Farley, too, was full of loyalty for his friend and fellow–classman, but he did not allow this to blind his judgment. Farley's opinion was that Dave was done for, unless he could land some lucky fluke in a knockout blow.

"Go right in and land that youngster," Treadwell's own seconds were advising him. "Don't let him have the satisfaction of standing up to you for three whole rounds or more."

"Do you think that little teaser is as easy as he looks?" growled Treadwell.

"Oh, Darrin is all right at his own weight," admitted Midshipman Conners. "But he has no business with you, Tread. You're quick enough, too, when you exert yourself. So jump right in and finish it before this round is over."

"I'll try it, then," nodded Treadwell.

Though he had not the slightest notion that he was to be defeated, this big top classman was learning a new respect for Darrin's prowess. He could thrash Dave, of course, but Treadwell did not expect to do it easily.

For the first twenty seconds of the third round the two men sparred cautiously. Dave had no relish for standing the full force of those sledge–hammer blows, while Treadwell knew that he must look out for the unexpected from his still nimble opponent.

"Lie down when you've had enough," jeered Treadwell, as he landed a jolt on one of the youngster's shoulders and sent him reeling slightly.

Dave, however, used his feet well enough to get away from the follow-up.

"Are you getting tired?" Darrin shot back at his opponent.

"Silence, both of you," commanded Referee Edgerton. "Do all your talking with your fists!"

Just then Treadwell saw an opening, and followed the referee's advice by aiming a blow at Dave's left jaw. It landed just back of the ear, instead, yet with such force that Dave sank dizzily to the ground, while Treadwell drew back from the intended follow-up.

Farley and Page looked on anxiously from their corner. Midshipman Wheeler, scanning his watch, was counting off the seconds.

"—five, six, seven, eight, nine—ten!"

At the sound of eight Dave Darrin had made a strenuous effort to rise.

Yet he had swayed, fallen back slightly, then forced himself with a rush to his feet.

But Midshipman Treadwell drew back, both fists hanging at his sides, for the "ten" had been spoken, and Dave Darrin had lost the count.

While Dave stood there, looking half-dizzily at his opponent, Referee Edgerton's voice broke in crisply:

"Mr. Darrin required more than the full count to come back. The fight is therefore awarded to Mr. Treadwell."

CHAPTER XVIII. FIGHTING THE FAMOUS DOUBLE BATTLE

"It wasn't fair," hissed Midshipman Page hotly.

"It was by a mighty small margin, anyway," quivered Farley.

"I don't feel whipped yet," remarked Dave quietly.

"Oh, well, Darry," urged Farley, "don't feel humiliated over being thrashed by such a human mountain of a top classer."

Dave, whose chest had been heaving, and whose lungs had been taking in great gulps of air, suddenly pushed his second gently away.

"Mr. Treadwell, sir, will you come over here a moment?" he called. "And also the officials of the fight?"

Treadwell, with a self−satisfied leer on his face, stepped away from his seconds coming jauntily over.

Midshipman Edgerton and Wheeler followed in some wonder.

"Mr. Treadwell," began Dave, looking full into the eyes of his late antagonist, "I have no fault, sir, to find with your style of fighting. You behaved fairly at every point."

"Thank you, sir," interjected the big midshipman grimly.

"The verdict was also fair enough," Dave continued, "for I am aware that I took a hair's−breadth more than the count. Still, I do not feel, Mr. Treadwell, that the result was decisive. Therefore I have to ask of you the favor of another early meeting, for a more definite try−out."

Treadwell gasped. So did his recent seconds and the late officials of the fight. Even Farley's jaw dropped just a trifle, but Page's face flushed with new−found pleasure.

"Another fight, sir?" demanded Midshipman Treadwell.

"Yes, sir," replied Darrin quietly.

"Oh, very well," agreed Treadwell, nonchalantly. "At any time that you wish, Mr. Darrin—any time."

"How would fifteen minutes from now do?" demanded Dave, smiling coolly.

Treadwell fairly gasped, though only from sheer astonishment.

"Why, if your seconds and the officials think that fair to you, Mr. Darrin," replied Treadwell in another moment, "I am sure that I have no objection to remaining around here a little longer."

"Do you insist on calling for the second fight within fifteen minutes, Mr. Darrin?" asked Second Classman Edgerton.

"For my own part, I do," replied Dave quietly; "I leave the decision to Mr. Treadwell's courtesy."

"Well, of all the freaks!" muttered Mr. Wheeler, as the two fight officials walked aside to discuss the matter.

"Darry," demanded the agitated Farley, "are you plumb, clean crazy?"

"Do you know what we're fighting about, Farley, old man?" asked Dave very quietly.

"No; of course not."

"It's a personal matter."

"O–oh!"

"It's a matter in which I can't accept an imitation whipping."

"But surely you don't expect to whip Treadwell in your present condition?"

"I very likely shall get a thorough trouncing," smiled Darrin.

"It's madness," broke in Page worriedly.

"I told you it was a personal matter," laughed Dave softly. "I shan't mind getting whacked if it is done up in good shape. It's only this near—whipping to which I object."

"Well—great Scott!" gasped Page.

"Hush!" warned Farley. "Here comes Edgerton."

Midshipman Edgerton, looking very much puzzled, stepped over to Dave Darrin's corner.

"Darrin," began the referee in a friendly tone, "Tread doesn't like the idea of fighting you again to—night."

"Didn't he say he would?" demanded Darrin.

"Yes; but of course, but—"

"I hold him to his word, Mr. Edgerton."

"But of all the crazy—"

"I have my own reasons, sir," Darrin interposed quietly. "I think it very likely, too, that Mr. Treadwell will comprehend my reasons."

"But he doesn't like the idea of fighting an already half—whipped man."

"Will it get on his nerves and unsteady him?" asked Dave ironically.

"Are you bound to fight to—night, Mr. Darrin?"

"I am, sir."

"Then I suppose it goes—it has to," assented Midshipman Edgerton moodily. "But of all the irrational—"

"Just what I said, sir," nodded Page.

"I shall be ready, sir, when the fifteen minutes are up," continued Dave. "But I am certain that I shall need all the time until then for getting myself into first–class condition."

"Darry is a fool—and a wonder!" ejaculated Edgerton under his breath, as he walked away.

"I'm sorry, Darry," murmured Farley mournfully, "but—well, beat your way to it!"

"I intend to," retorted Dave doggedly.

Rubbed down by his seconds, Dave drew on his blouse, without a shirt.

Quitting the others, Dave walked briskly back and forth. At last he broke into a jog–trot.

At last he halted, inflating and emptying his lungs with vigorous breathing.

"I feel just about as good as ever," he declared, nodding cheerily to his seconds.

"Get off that blouse, then," ordered Midshipman Farley, after a glance at his watch. "We've two minutes left out of the fifteen."

"I'll go forward at the scratch, then," nodded Dave.

Treadwell, in the meantime, had pulled on his outer clothing and had stood moodily by, watching Dave's more workmanlike preparations with a disdainful smile.

"I'll get the fellow going quickly this time," Mr. Treadwell told Conners. "As soon as I get him going I'll dive in with a punch that will wind up the matter in short order. I've planned to do considerable reviewing of navigation to–night."

"I hope you have your wish," murmured Conners.

"What do you mean?"

"Just what I said."

"Do you think I'm going to have any trouble whatever about finishing up that touge youngster!" demanded Tread well sarcastically.

"No; I don't imagine you will. But at the same time, Tread, I tell you I don't care about having enemies among fellows who come back as swiftly, strongly and as much like a bulldog as Darry does."

Seeing Dave pull off his blouse, Treadwell slowly removed his own clothing above the waist.

"Rub me down along the arms a bit," said Midshipman Treadwell, after he had exercised his arms a moment.

"I reckon we'd better," nodded Conners. "You must have got stiff from standing still after the late mix–up."

"No kinks but what will iron out at once," chuckled Treadwell. "I'll show you as soon as I get in action."

His two seconds rubbed him down loyally.

"Are you ready, gentlemen?" called Midshipman Edgerton.

Both men stepped quickly forward, but all of the onlookers thought they saw rather more spring in Dave Darrin than in his more bulky opponent.

The preliminaries were announced in a few words.

Of course, there was no handshaking.

"Time!" sounded the call.

Dave Darrin quickly proved to be so full of vigor that Treadwell lay back on the defensive after the first two or three passes. Dave followed him right up with vim.

Yet, for the first forty seconds of the round no real damage was done on either side. Then:

Bump!

"O–o–oh!"

That cry came simultaneously from Treadwell and from all the spectators.

Dave's right fist had landed crushingly on the top classman's left eye, almost instantly closing that organ.

Darrin leaped nimbly back, both from a chivalrous impulse to give Treadwell a chance to recover his steadiness and to save himself from any sudden rush and clinch by his big opponent.

But Treadwell, standing with his guard up, showed no inclination to follow the one who had just given him such punishment.

"Mix it up, gentlemen—mix it!" called Midshipman Edgerton impatiently.

At that command from the referee Dave Darrin sprang forward.

Treadwell seemed wholly on the defensive now, though he struck as heavily as ever. Toward the end of the round Treadwell, having gotten over the worst of the stinging from his eye, once more tried to rush matters.

Whenever the big fellow's undamaged eye caught sight of the cool, hostile smile on Darrin's face, Treadwell muttered savage words.

Some hard body blows were parried and others exchanged.

Both men were panting somewhat when the call of time closed the first round.

"Darry, you nervy little rascal, waltz in and put that other eye up in black clothes!" begged Page ecstatically, as he and Farley worked over their principal.

Dave was ready quite twenty seconds before the call of time for the second round.

Treadwell, however, took his full time in responding. At the last moment he took another dab with the wet sponge against his swollen left eye.

"Time!"

With a suppressed yell Treadwell rushed at his opponent. Dave had to sidestep to his own right, out of range of Treadwell, to save himself.

Then at it they went, all around the ring. Darrin had determined to keep himself out of the way of those sledge–hammer fists until he saw his own clear opening.

Four or five times Treadwell landed heavily on Darrin's ribs. The younger, smaller midshipman was getting seriously winded, but all the time he fought to save himself and to get that one opening.

It came.

Pound!

Darrin's hard–clenched left fist dropped in on Treadwell's right eye.

This time there was no exclamation from the bruised one.

Alert Dave was careful to give him no chance. Within a second after that eye–closer landed Darrin struck with his right, landing on the jaw bone under Treadwell's ear.

Down in a heap sank the top classman. He was unconscious before his body struck the ground.

Wheeler counted off the seconds.

"—ten!"

Still Mr. Treadwell lay motionless.

"Do your best for him, gentlemen," begged Referee Edgerton, turning to the first classman's seconds. "Mr. Darrin wins the second fight."

Dave, a satisfied look on his face, stepped back to his seconds.

This time he did not require as much attention. Within five minutes he was dressed.

By this time Mr. Treadwell, under the ministrations of his seconds and of the late officials, was just coming back to consciousness.

"Something happened, eh?" asked the top classman drowsily.

"Rather!" murmured Mr. Edgerton dryly.

"Did I—did I—lose the fight?"

"You did," Edgerton assented. "But don't let that disturb you. You went down before the best man in the Naval Academy."

Treadwell sighed gloomily. It was a hard blow to his pride—much harder than any that Dave had landed on his head.

"Mr. Treadwell," inquired Dave, stepping over, "we are comrades, even if we had a slight disagreement. Do you care to shake hands?"

"Help me to my feet," urged the first classman, who was sitting up.

His seconds complied. Then Midshipman Treadwell held out his hand.

"Here's my hand," he said rather thickly. "And I apologize, too, Mr. Darrin."

"Then say no more about it, please," begged Dave, as their hands met in a strong clasp.

None of the others present had the least idea of the provocation of this strange, spirited double fight. All, however, were glad to see the difficulty mended.

Then Dave and his seconds, leaving the field first, made their way back to Bancroft Hall. Farley and Page went straight to their own room.

"How did it come out?" demanded Dan Dalzell eagerly, as soon as his chum entered their quarters.

Dropping into a chair, Dave told the story of the double fight briefly. He told it modestly, too, but Dan could imagine what his chum omitted.

"David, little giant," exclaimed Dalzell, leaping about him, "that fight will become historic here! Oh, how I regret having missed it. Don't you ever dare to leave me out again!"

"It wasn't such a much," smiled Dave rather wearily, as he went over to his study desk.

"Perhaps it's indiscreet, even of a chum," rambled on Dalzell, "but what—"

"What was the fight all about?" laughed Dave softly. "Yes; I suppose you have a right to know that, Danny boy. But you must never repeat it to any one. Treadwell wanted to dance with Belle at the hop, but she had already noticed him, and declared she didn't want to dance with him. Of course that settled it. But Treadwell accused me of not having asked Belle."

"The nerve !" ejaculated Dan in disgust.

"And then he accused me of lying when I declared I had done my best for him," continued Dave.

"I feel that I'd like to fight the fellow myself!" declared Dan Dalzell hotly.

"Oh, no, you don't; for Treadwell apologized to–night, and we have shaken hands. We're all comrades, you know, Danny boy."

* * * * *

Unknown to any of the parties to the fight, there had been spectators of the spirited double battle.

Two men, a sailor and a marine, noting groups of midshipmen going toward the historic battle ground of midshipmen, had hidden themselves near-by in order "to see the fun."

These two enlisted men of the Navy had been spectators and auditors of all that had taken place.

Not until the last midshipman had left the ground did the sailor and marine emerge from their hiding place.

"Well, of all the game fights!" muttered the marine.

"Me? I'm hoping that some day I fight under that gallant middy," cried the sailor.

"Who is this Mr. Darrin?" asked the marine, as the pair strolled away.

"He's a youngster—third classman. But he's one of the chaps who, on the cruise, last summer, went over into a gale after another middy—Darrin and his chum did it."

"There must be fine stuff in Mr. Darrin," murmured the marine.

"Couldn't you see that much just now?" demanded the sailor, who took the remark as almost a personal affront, "My hat's off to Mr. Darrin. He's one of our future admirals. If I round out my days in the service it will be the height of my ambition to have him for my admiral. And a mighty sea-going officer he'll be, at that!"

In their enthusiasm over the spectacle they had seen, the sailor and the marine talked rather too much.

They were still talking over the battle as they strolled slowly past one of the great, darkened buildings.

In the shadow of this building, not far away, stood an officer whom neither of the enlisted men of the Navy saw; else they would have saluted him.

That officer, Lieutenant Willow, U.S. Navy, listened with a good deal of interest.

Mr. Willow was one of those officers who are known as duty–mad. He gathered that there had been a fight, so he deemed it his duty to report the fact at once to the discipline officer in charge over at Bancroft Hall.

Regretting the necessity, yet full of the idea of doing his duty, Lieutenant Willow wended his way promptly towards the office of the officer in charge.

CHAPTER XIX. THE OFFICER IN CHARGE IS SHOCKED

Through the main entrance of Bancroft Hall, into the stately corridor, Lieutenant Willow picked his way.

He looked solemn—unusually so, even for Lieutenant Willow, U.S.N. He had the air of a man who hates to do his duty, but who is convinced that the heavens would fall if he didn't.

To his left he turned, acknowledging smartly the crisp salute given him by the midshipman assistant officer of the day.

Into the outer office of the officer in charge stepped Mr. Willow, and thence on into the smaller room where Lieutenant–Commander Stearns sat reading.

"Oh, good evening, Willow," hailed Lieut. Stearns heartily.

"Good evening, Stearns," was the almost moody reply.

"Sit down and let's have a chat I'm glad to see you," urged Lieutenant–Commander Stearns.

Mr. Stearns, he of the round, jovial face, gazed at his junior with twinkling eyes.

"Willow," he muttered, "I'm half inclined to believe that you've come to me to make an official report."

"I guess I have," nodded Lieutenant Willow.

"And against some unfortunate midshipman, at that!"

"Against two, at least," sighed Mr. Willow, "and there were others involved in the affair."

"It must be something fearful," said Mr. Stearns, who knew the junior officer's inclination to be duty—mad. "But, see here, if you make an official report you'll force me to take action, even though it's something that I'd secretly slap a midshipman on the shoulder for doing. No—don't begin to talk yet, Willow. Try a cigar and then tell me, personally, what's worrying you. Then perhaps it won't be altogether needful to make an official report."

"I never was able to take you—er—somewhat jovial views of an officer's duty, Stearns," sighed Lieutenant Willow.

Nevertheless, he selected a cigar, bit off the end, lighted it and took a few whiffs, Lieutenant—Commander Stearns all the while regarding his comrade in arms with twinkling eyes.

"Now, fire ahead, Willow," urged the officer in charge, "but please don't make your communication an official one—not at first. Fire ahead, now, Willow."

"Well—er—just between ourselves," continued Lieutenant Willow slowly, "there has been a fight to—night between two midshipmen."

"No!"

Lieutenant—Commander Stearns struck his fist rather heavily against the desk.

"A fight—a real fight—with fists?" continued the officer in charge, in a tone of mock incredulity. "No, no, no, Willow, you don't mean it—you can't mean it!"

"Yes, I do," rejoined the junior officer rather stiffly.

"Oh, dear, what is the service coming to?" gasped Stearns ironically. "Why, Willow, we never heard of such things when we were midshipmen here. Now, did we?"

"I'm afraid we did—sometimes," admitted the junior officer. "But duty is duty, you know, my dear Stearns. And this was an unusual fight, too. The man who was whipped insisted on another fight right then and there, and—he won the second fight."

"Bully!" chuckled the officer in charge. "Whew, but I wish I had been there!"

"Stearns, you surely don't mean that?" gasped duty–mad Mr. Willow.

"You're quite right, Willow. No; I certainly don't want to be a spoilsport, and I'm glad I wasn't there—in my official capacity. But I'd like to have been divested of my rank for just an hour so that I could have taken in such a scene as that."

"I'm—I'm just a bit astonished at your saying it, Stearns," rejoined Lieutenant Willow. "But then, you're always joking."

"Perhaps I am joking," assented the officer in charge dryly, "but I never lose sight of the fact that our Navy has been built up, at huge expense, as a great fighting machine. Now, Willow, it takes fighting men to run a fighting machine. Of course, I'm terribly shocked to know that two midshipmen really had the grit to fight—but who were they! Mind you, I'm not asking you in an official way. This question is purely personal—just between ourselves. Who were the men? And, especially, who was the fellow who lost the decision, and then had the utter effrontery to demand a second chance at once, only to win the second fight?"

"Darrin was the man who lost the first fight and won the second," replied Lieutenant Willow.

"Mr. Darrin? One of our youngsters! Yes; I think I know him. And what man of his class did he whip, the second time he tried!"

"It wasn't a man of his own class. It was Mr. Treadwell, of the first class," rejoined Lieutenant Willow.

"What?" almost exploded the officer in charge. "Did you say that Mr. Darrin fought with Mr. Treadwell, that husky top classman, and, losing the decision on the count, insisted on fighting again the same evening? Oh, say, what a fellow misses by being cooped up in an office like this!"

"But—but the breach of regulations!" stammered the duty-mad lieutenant.

"My dear fellow, neither you nor I know anything about this fight—officially. The Navy, after all, is a fighting machine. Do you feel that the Navy can afford to lose a fighting man like that youngster?"

So Lieutenant Willow left Lieutenant-Commander Stearns' presence, not quite convinced he was performing his whole duty, but glad to bow to the decision of a ranking officer.

Two days later Dave and Dan were surprised at being halted by Lieutenant-Commander Stearns.

"Good afternoon, Mr. Darrin," came the pleasant greeting. "Good afternoon, Mr. Dalzell. Mrs. Stearns and I would be greatly pleased if you could take dinner with us. Couldn't you come next Sunday?"

The two midshipmen were astonished and delighted at this invitation. While it was not uncommon for officers to invite midshipmen to their homes, where there were so many midshipmen, it was as a rule only the young men who made themselves prominent socially who captured these coveted invitations. Darrin and Dalzell concealed their surprise, but expressed their pleasure in accepting the gracious invitation.

On entering Mrs. Stearns' drawing room the next Sunday Mr. Darrin and Mr. Dalzell were introduced to two pretty girls. Miss Flora Gentle was a cousin of their hostess. She had visited Annapolis before, and, being pretty and vivacious, at the same time kind and considerate, she had many friends among the midshipmen. Marian Stevens, who had accompanied her on this visit, was a direct contrast. Flora was blonde. Marian was the dark, flashing type. She was spoiled and imperious, yet she had a dashing, open way about her that made her a favorite among young people.

The two girls had heard of the double fight. Marian, therefore, was pleased when she found that Dave was to be her dinner partner.

"He's handsome," thought the girl, "and he's brave and dashing. He'll make his mark in the Navy. He doesn't know it yet, but he'll become mine, and mine alone."

Miss Stevens was a calculating young person, and had already decided that Navy life was the life for her and that she would marry into it. At seventeen, she looked upon the officers as old men, even the youngest of them, so was giving her time and her smiles to the midshipmen. That the Navy pay is small did not trouble Maid Marian, as she liked to be called, as on her twenty−first birthday she would come into a considerable fortune of her own.

She exerted herself all through the Stearns' dinner to captivate Dave Darrin. He, without diminution of love and loyalty to Belle Mead, was glad to be on friendly terms with this dashing and sprightly girl.

Coffee was served in the drawing room. Several officers dropped in. Marian, who wished no one to come between her and Dave for a while, turned to her host.

"Mr. Stearns, do the regulations make it improper for Flora and me to ask Mr. Darrin and Mr. Dalzell to take us for a stroll about the yard?" she asked with a pretty air of deference. The "yard" includes all the grounds belonging to the Naval Academy.

"They do not, Miss Marian," was the smiling response.

"With our hostess's approval we shall be charmed to grant any request the young ladies make," ventured Dave, as Marian smiled into his eyes.

But Marian, the wily and experienced, found herself baffled during this walk. Using all her cajoleries, she could bring him to a certain point beyond which he would not go. As a matter of fact, Dave Darrin, secure in his loyalty to Belle, did not perceive what Maid Marian was striving to lead up to, but saw in her only a lively and interesting girl.

"I'll get you yet, Midshipman Darrin," she vowed to herself after they had parted.

The gossip of a sweetheart in his home town which in time reached her ears only made the girl more determined to get her way. Looking in the mirror with satisfaction, she murmured:

"There'll be the added zest of making Midshipman Darrin forget the distant face of that home girl."

Not on that visit did Maid Marian succeed in leading Dave beyond the point of simple but sincere friendship. However, Miss Stevens could be charming to whomsoever she wished, and before she left Annapolis she had secured invitations to visit the wife of more than one of the officers.

CHAPTER XX. CONCLUSION

Christmas came and went, and soon after this the semi−annual examinations were on in earnest. Some of the midshipmen failed and sadly turned their faces homeward to make a place for themselves in some other lane of life. Dan Dalzell, however, made good his promise, and by a better margin than he had dared hope. Dave came through the examination somewhat better than his chum. Both felt assured now that they would round out the year with fair credit to themselves.

Marian Stevens came to Annapolis several times during the latter half of the year, and as it is expected that the future officer shall have social as well as Naval training, Dave Darrin met her often.

Exasperation that she could draw the young midshipman on only so far soon changed in Miss Stevens to anger and chagrin. Still Dave, giving prolonged thought to no girl except Belle Meade, saw in her only a lively companion. Sometimes he was her dinner partner. Always at a dance he danced with her more than once.

It was at one such dance that she looked up as they circled the room to say:

"I wonder if you know, Mr. Darrin, how much I enjoy dancing with you."

"Not as much as I enjoy dancing with you," he replied smilingly. Just then the music stopped suddenly and an officer called in a voice that carried over the great floor of the gymnasium and over all the chatter:

"Ladies and gentlemen, one moment's attention, please!"

In an instant all was still.

"Ladies and gentlemen," continued the officer, "official permission has been granted for taking a flashlight photograph of the scene to–night. Will everybody please remain where he is until after the exposure has been made?"

Dave and Marian had paused directly in front of the lens of the camera. Maid Marian looked up and made a light, jesting remark, gazing straight into the midshipman's eyes. Dave, smiling, bent forward to hear what she said.

Just then came the flash, and the photographer, his work finished for the time, gathered his paraphernalia together and left. The music recommenced and the dancing proceeded.

Three weeks later that photograph was reproduced as a double–page illustration in one of the prominent pictorial weeklies.

The day the magazine was on the newsstands Dan Dalzell bought a copy. Entering their quarters with it in his hand he opened it at the illustration and handed it to Dave.

"You and Miss Stevens show up better than any one else, Dave," remarked Dan.

"The photograph is a good piece of work," was Dave's only comment. He did not wish to express the annoyance he felt when he noted the appearance of intimacy between him and Marian, whose beauty showed, even in this reproduction. "I'd a bit rather Belle shouldn't see this paper," he admitted to himself.

"David, old boy, this picture would make a good exhibit in a breach–of–promise suit."

"That's an unkind remark to make about a fine girl like Miss Stevens," said Dave coldly.

Dan stared, then went off, pondering.

Belle Meade, in her Gridley home, received one day a large, square, thin package. She saw the mark of the Annapolis express office, and hastily snatched up scissors to cut the string. Out came a huge photograph.

"A picture of an Annapolis dance! How thoughtful of Dave to send it to me!" Then her eyes fell on two figures around which a ring had been drawn in ink. They were Dave Darrin and a pretty girl. On the margin of the card had been scrawled in bold letters:

"Your affair of the heart will bear close watching if you still cherish!"

This was signed, contemptibly and untruthfully, "A Friend."

"Uh!" murmured Belle in hurt pride and loyalty. Then she said resolutely to herself: "I will pay no attention to this. An anonymous communication is always meant to hurt and to give a false impression."

But there was the picture before her eyes of Dave and the pretty girl in seemingly great intimacy. So though she continued to write to the midshipman and tried hard to make her letters sound as usual, in spite of herself a coldness crept into them that Dave felt.

"She must have seen that pictorial weekly," thought the boy miserably. But as Belle said nothing of this, he could not write of it.

The season was well along. Dave and Dan sent Belle Meade and Laura Bentley invitations to one of the later spring dances.

"I wonder if she'll come or if she's tiring of me," thought Dave Darrin bitterly.

But Belle answered, accepting the invitation for Laura and herself.

When Saturday afternoon came both midshipmen hurried to the hotel in the town and sent up their cards. Mrs. Meade soon appeared, saying the girls would be down shortly.

"Are they both well?" asked Dave. His tone was as one giving a meaningless greeting, but in his heart he waited anxiously to hear what her mother should say of Belle.

"Well, yes. But Belle has been moping around the house a great deal, Dave, rather unlike her usual self," replied Mrs. Meade slowly.

If Mrs. Meade deplored this, Dave Darrin did not. It showed him at least that the girl's apparent coldness was not caused by her interest in some other young man.

But when the girls came in and Belle greeted him cordially, to be sure, but with something of restraint, his heart sank again.

"What's the matter, Belle? Has something gone wrong?" asked Dave when Dan was engaging the attention of Mrs. Meade and Laura.

"Nothing. Is all right with you?"

"Surely!"

"Dave, when we're alone I have something to show you. I fear you have an enemy here."

"An enemy! Oh, no. But I shall be glad to see what you have to show me."

It was not long before, at a word from Dave, Dan took Mrs. Meade and Laura out for a walk. It was then that Belle got the large photograph with the two figures ringed in ink and showed it to Dave.

"Why, what does this mean? Some one must have taken a good deal of trouble to secure this photograph. The picture was taken for a pictorial weekly. One can get a photograph from which the cut is made, but it is troublesome and possibly expensive!"

"You have an enemy, then; some one bent on hurting you?"

"I don't know who it could be. My, how angry Miss Stevens would be if she knew of this!"

"Miss Stevens? Is that the girl?"

"Yes. She's visited here often this year. She knows a number of the officers' wives. She's vivacious and always has a good time, but she's nothing to me, Belle. You know that, don't you?"

"I have never doubted you, Dave. Let us tear this up. I thought at first I'd not show it to you; then decided it was best not to begin concealing things from you. But let us not think of the thing again."

"Belle, you're a thoroughbred!" and here the matter dropped as far as it was between Dave Darrin and Belle Meade.

Miss Stevens was at the dance that evening. Though she tried hard to make that impossible, Dave did not dance with her, nor did he introduce her to Belle, though there again Marian tried to force this.

It would have been well for Marian if Dan Dalzell had been equally circumspect.

This time it was Belle who contrived and got the introduction to the other girl, but Marian was by no means reluctant, so it was that they managed to get a few moments alone together when they had sent their dance partners to get something for them.

"You are a friend of Dave's, aren't you?" asked Marian.

"Of Mr. Darrin's? Oh, yes, we've always known each other."

"Then you've been here to many of these dances?"

"Only two."

"Too bad you could not have been here oftener. This has been an unusually brilliant season. Really, many of the young people have lost their heads—or their hearts. I often wonder if these midshipmen have sweethearts at home." This daring—and impertinent—remark was made musingly but smilingly.

"These Annapolis affairs are never very serious, I imagine," Belle observed calmly.

"On the contrary, most of the Navy marriages date back to an Annapolis first meeting."

"Then you think it well to come often?"

"Unless one has other ways of keeping in touch," was the brazen reply.

"I have," said Belle sweetly. "I receive a good many souvenirs in the course of a year. One last winter was a photograph." With the words Belle gazed intently into Miss Stevens' eyes. Then she went on: "There was an anonymous message written on it. It was a lying message, of course, as anonymous messages always are, written in a coarse hand. Did you ever study handwriting, Miss Stevens?"

Marian gasped, realizing she was out–maneuvered.

"This writing had all the characteristics of a woman whose instincts are coarse, that of a treacherous though not dangerous person—"

"Here's Mr. Sanderson back. Will you excuse me, Miss Meade?" and Marian fairly fled.

Belle told Dave she had found out who had sent the photograph, but added:

"I wish you wouldn't ask me who it was, Dave. I can assure you that the person who did it will never trouble us again," and as Dave did not like to think evil of any one, he consented, and continued to think of Marian Stevens, when he thought of her at all, as a jolly girl.

The annual examinations were approaching. Dan Dalzell was buried deep in gloom. Dave Darrin kept cheerful outwardly, but doubts crept into his heart.

The examinations over, Dave felt reasonably safe. But Dan's gloom deepened, for he was sure he had failed in "skinny," as the boys termed chemistry and physics. So it was that when the grades were posted Dave scanned the D's in the list of third classmen who had passed. Dan, on the other hand, turned instantly to what he termed the "bust list."

"Why, why, I'm not there!" he muttered.

"Look at the passing list, Danny," laughed Dave.

Unbelieving, Dan turned his eyes on the list and to his utter astonishment found his name posted. True, in "skinny" he had a bare passing mark. But in other subjects he was somewhat above the minimum.

"So you see, old man, we'll both be here next year as second classmen," said Dave jubilantly.

This was as Dave Darrin said, and what happened during this time may be learned in a volume entitled, "DAVE DARRIN'S THIRD YEAR AT ANNAPOLIS; or, Leaders of the Second Class Midshipmen."

THE END

Printed in the United States
19733LVS00002B/130